BEDTIME STORIES FOR CARRION BEETLES

*For Carol and Scott —
Happy Halloween!*

ADRIAN LUDENS

All rights reserved. No part of this book may be reproduced or transmitted in any form or by electronic or mechanical means without the written permission of the author and/or publisher.

This is a work of fiction. Names, characters, places and incidents are either products of the author's imagination or are used fictitiously. Any resemblance to actual persons, living or dead, events or locales is entirely coincidental.

Cover photo: Heidi Ludens, 1229gallery@gmail.com
Author photo: Ashley Brechtel

Copyright © 2012 Adrian W. Ludens
All rights reserved.
ISBN: 1463722664
ISBN-13: 978-1463722661

DEDICATION

To my wife, Crissy. Thank you for your patience. To my children: Maddy, Victor, Ashley, and Taylor: Thanks for hanging in there when Dad went A.W.O.L. ("absent without leaving") in order to write. This collection is also dedicated to those who own a copy of either of my first two "homemade" collections. Thank you all. Special thanks to my fellow writers in the Horror Writers Association and in Black Hills Writers Group. In particular, I'd like to thank Lisa Morton, Ty Schwamberger and Ken Lillie-Paetz for their advice and support, and Karen Hall and Michaelia Kendall for editing large portions of the manuscript.

CONTENTS

Acknowledgments	i
A Good Game	7
You Don't Know Jack	16
Carrying On	36
Swollen Tick	39
Tomorrow's Headline	54
Solitary Man	63
Wind, Winter, Wendigo	68
Cold Feet	81
Transformations	94
Incident on Alkali Road	102
The Red Patch in the Snow	118
The Restoration Room	122
Hydrophobia	139
A Story About Monsters	148
The Artist and His Subject	152
There's No Word For It	164
Bootlegs From Boston	175
The Biggin Hill Duel	193
Waiting for Inspiration	213

ADRIAN LUDENS

A GOOD GAME

The malignant odor made him feel like vomiting. He opened his eyes but saw only darkness, which was the same as seeing nothing at all. He flexed his fingers experimentally and found them swollen and slow to respond. Still, he could move, so he mentally checked 'coma' off his list of possible scenarios. Though it was dark and he seemed to be at rest, he felt as if he were standing.

Where am I?

He realized he didn't know.

What's my name?

Rockwell. Yes. That much he knew. Rockwell Allen. He was 'Rocky' to his friends. He was a wealthy man, a powerful man. Rocky was A Success Story. Yet he was still in the dark, literally and figuratively.

Rocky's veins should have been coursing with indignant wrath over his current predicament, but he felt curiously placid. He couldn't seem to motivate his body into action. If he vomited on himself in reaction to the odor, so be it. Rocky waited, quietly gazing into the blackness. He did this for a period of several minutes. Just when Rocky realized he hadn't blinked yet, light assailed his eyes.

"You, in the box," a voice intoned. It was a young voice, consciously dropped into a lower register to sound older. "Tell us your name." There was a titter and the sound of jostling from somewhere behind him.

"Rocky Allen." He could barely whisper the words. *Laryngitis?*

"Come out of there, Rocky," the voice instructed.

Rocky awkwardly moved his feet and lurched out of his confinement. He found himself in a large room, dark and dank. Someone had haphazardly piled boxes into the corner to his left in an apparent effort to clear floor space. Black plastic garbage bags with misshapen contents lay near a square steel door to his right. *A kiln? Industrial oven?* Rocky didn't know. A woman stood before him. She was beautiful; a brunette with an olive complexion, wearing an expensive looking dress with a modest cut. On the floor between him and the woman lay an assortment of lawn and garden equipment, and the contents of a tool box. He wanted to greet the woman but something felt off-kilter. It seemed to Rocky that he couldn't move or speak without direction.

"This is Vanessa D'Angelo," the voice from earlier piped up from the darkness. "She's contestant number one. Rocky Allen, you're contestant number two." A flicker of recognition kindled dimly in Rocky's muddled brain. *Vanessa? My new assistant at the office?*

"I want to spend my life with you," he whispered in her ear.

Vanessa sighed and stretched languidly. Her smoldering gaze elated him, made him love life again. She rolled over onto him and pinned his arms to the bed. "Prove it," she challenged.

Rocky bit his lip and worked his hips. She was easily the most gorgeous woman he had ever laid eyes upon.

"Say my name," she begged.

"Vanessa," This voice was new and higher-pitched than the first. "Pick up the shovel from the floor."

Vanessa stooped and picked up a spade. The voices argued briefly from behind Rocky, conferring in excited whispers. One side apparently won out and he heard the second, higher voice say, "That's a spade, but close enough." Vanessa looked baffled but did not speak.

"Now hit that man with the spade," the second voice commanded.

Rocky tried stepping back into the safe-feeling confines he had come from but couldn't find the energy to move. It was if his shoes had been glued to the floor. Vanessa edged toward him and finally stopped about four feet away. She swung the spade. Rocky watched it come.

The broad side of the blade struck his shoulder with a muffled thump. Rocky was relieved that she hadn't hurt him. He tried to furrow his brow in admonition without success.

"Do it again, but harder this time," the first voice said.

"And aim at his head," the second added.

Vanessa swung and Rocky heard a flat, atonal burst of sound.

A wallop. That's what he'd heard. *A real wallop. Like during a car accident.*

Rocky realized that he'd gotten shorter. Or perhaps Vanessa had grown in stature somehow. He heard giggles.

Rocky realized he was kneeling on the dirty concrete. His suit jacket felt like it had completely torn down the back. Or had it been that way to begin with?

"Get up, Rocky." He got up.

"Pick up the hammer." Rocky's body followed the directions despite his mental reservations. He crouched and picked up a rusty claw hammer.

"Now hit that woman," the higher voice directed. "With the claw side."

Rocky awkwardly swung the hammer. He missed Vanessa almost completely. The claw managed to catch on the front of her dress however, tearing it down the middle.

Rocky stood staring at the large black letter 'Y' stitched across the dusky skin of her chest and stomach.

She was in a car accident. Rocky realized. *We were in the same car. Where were we coming from?*

"We'll just tell anyone who asks it was a business luncheon," Rocky said.

Vanessa leaned back against the seat, a smirk playing at her lips. "If the people you work with are dumb enough to believe that, then I should be the CEO in six months."

Rocky glanced at her. "If I get my wish, you'll be Mrs. Rockwell Allen in six months."

His companion rolled her eyes and favored him with a pixie-like smile. "Then I'll be able to stop calling you Mr. Allen and start calling you-"

"Rocky! I want you to swing again with the hammer side and aim for her face," a voice said. Rocky swung the hammer again. There was a muffled crack as the head of the makeshift weapon connected with her nose and mashed it to the left, against her cheek. Yellowish fluid dribbled from her nostrils.

Rocky mentally shrieked his apologies to Vanessa, but his mouth remained silent. His jaw felt wired shut. Vanessa showed no signs of agony or even dismay.

"Let go of the hammer." Rocky let his arm drop to his side. The hammer clanked on the concrete.

"I'm still gonna win," the higher voice vowed.

The other speaker gave only a derisive snort in response.

The higher voice called Vanessa's name again. "Pick up the pliers." The woman obeyed.

"Pull his left ear off."

Rocky wished he could run away. A set of stairs crouched in the dimness of the far wall. If he could regain control of his body, he could scoop up Vanessa in his arms and carry her to safety like a groom carries his bride across the threshold.

By now Vanessa had clamped down on his earlobe with the pliers and had started to pull. The lobe tore free abruptly and Vanessa's arm jerked away.

"Grab it from the top," the higher voice instructed. Vanessa complied and Rocky felt his head being pulled toward her. Again, her beauty struck him. *I think I fell in love with this woman...*

Vanessa's hand slid up his thigh. Rocky, dimly aware of sirens, gazed in the rear view mirror for the source. His world became one of polished red and gleaming chrome as a fire department ladder truck slammed into the side of the Lincoln at full speed. Buildings, people and other vehicles spun crazily around him. The sound of the impact was what Rocky had always imagined a stick of dynamite would sound like when it detonated. Then he heard the shriek of tearing metal. Another shriek followed. *Vanessa.*

Rocky turned his head to look at her and a sharp pain shot through his neck. He cried out. Her eyes were wide, and blood dribbled from her nose and ears. Vanessa's hands shook as she reached out for him.

"Oh my God," she sobbed.

Keeping his eyes open became too much of an effort and he let them slide closed. He heard Vanessa repeating his name.

"Rocky. Rocky! Stand up straight," the higher voice commanded.

Rocky followed his instructions and a tearing reverberated in his head. It was the sound of one thousand Velcro strips ripping under water.

Vanessa stood staring idly at her hand and at the pinkish-white object caught in the grip of the pliers. "It kinda looks like a seashell," the higher voice remarked.

"Rocky, pick up the lawn mower blade." The lower voice shook Rocky from a blank reverie. He scanned the floor until he saw the blade. Half of it had been thickly wrapped with duct tape to create a handle of sorts. Rocky stooped to pick it up.

"Off with her head!" The voice commanded. He swung his arm in a wide arc toward the object of his affection. The sharp side of the blade buried itself halfway through Vanessa's tan neck.

"Again!"

Stop making me do this!

Rocky's right arm worked the blade free and he swung again. A wet butcher's block sound rebounded from the dank walls as the vertebrate and spinal cord were severed.

"Again!"

Jesus! Why can't I stop?

On his third swing, Rocky's blade sliced through his lover's neck completely, and Vanessa's head landed on the concrete with a flat thud. The room was filled with the enthusiastic applause of two pairs of small hands. *I'm sorry Vanessa. I hope you are in a better place now.*

"My guy won!" The lower voice announced excitedly.

"This is a pretty fun game," the higher one declared. "We should go get more and play again."

"What's all de noise?" An ancient, quavering voice demanded suddenly from the shadowy staircase. "What chu doin' down heah'?"

Thank God! Finally some help...

"Hang on sir, we're here to help." Rocky had been floating in a soothing sea of darkness when the urgent voice shocked him into awareness. He hurt. Everywhere. Why was this guy bothering him? Rocky opened his eyes. Everything seemed too bright and tinted with crimson so he closed them again.

"Stay with me, sir," the paramedic's voice grated his ears again. "You've got to stay awake. Why don't you tell me your name?"

Rocky kept his mouth closed tight. He was too tired to make the effort and said...

"Nothing!" The lower voice spoke.

"Yeah, nothing Gran," piped the higher one.

"Just playin' is all!" the self-proclaimed winner added.

An elderly, frail-looking woman hobbled down two more stairs. Her gnarled hands never left the security of the worn banister. Rocky made out her features more clearly. A myriad of wrinkles made her dark face look like an ancient parchment map. Milky cataracts webbed across her eyes. Rocky's hopes fell. *Yell at her for help!* Rocky knew it was useless but he tried anyway.

Nothing happened.

"Well, come *fè twalèt*-wash up," she croaked. Her Creole-Haitian accent was so thick Rocky had a hard time understanding her words. "You can finish your *jwèt*- after we eat." The old woman turned and trudged slowly back up the stairs.

"Gran, can we play outside after dinner?" asked the higher voice.

"*Non pitit*, I heard on de radio 'bout someone snatchin' bodies from de funeral parlor. That's bad hoodoo happening jus' up de street an' I don't want either of you out in de dark."

"Yes, Gran," the voices chorused dutifully.

"We'll be right up," the lower voiced one promised. The ancient woman's spindly legs disappeared.

"Finish chopping her up," the speaker hissed, now quite close to Rocky's remaining ear. "Then bag up the parts and carry them over there." A slender arm pointed past Rocky toward the square steel door. *Not a kiln or an oven,* Rocky realized dimly. *An incinerator.*

"Then get back in your box," the voice finished. Rocky watched with vague interest as two slight forms brushed past him and moved toward the stairs. The boy put his arm around his younger sister's shoulders and squeezed.

"Good game," he said.

Rocky carried out his orders, hurling a barrage of useless apologies at Vanessa's memory all the while. He finally shambled back toward his box which leaned against the back wall. It was an oblong-shaped affair of plywood sheets crudely nailed together in the rough approximation of a casket. Rocky saw for the first time juice boxes and candy wrappers strewn around two sun-faded lawn chairs sitting nearby. Leaning against one of the chairs was a tall wooden staff decorated with bones, feathers and other objects Rocky could not identify. He felt as if a light electrical current were flowing through him when he looked at it. He stepped closer but the sensation became one of extreme discomfort. The boy's last command needled his brain. Rocky abandoned the strange-looking staff and instead climbed back into his box and closed the lid. The buzzing discomfort subsided. Rocky wondered about the incinerator. *If I got close enough, could I burn? Could I leave this place? If I do, might Vanessa be there to greet me?*

BEDTIME STORIES FOR CARRION BEETLES

Standing at rest in his box, Rocky flexed his fingers experimentally and found them swollen and slow to respond. His eyes were open but he saw only darkness, which was the same as seeing nothing at all. The malignant odor made him feel like vomiting.

# YOU DON'T KNOW JACK

The dead boy stood in the path twenty yards ahead. Jack pulled on the reins of his dun and the animal halted. The sun beat down mercilessly, and Jack paused to mop his brow with a threadbare red handkerchief. He rolled a quirley and surveyed his surroundings. To his left he saw only an endless expanse of rolling Dakota Territory prairie; to his right was more of the same. His direction took him toward the Black Hills, crouching on the distant horizon.

Jack squinted back at the ghost. Andy, eternally youthful, motioned with one transparent arm for the rider to leave the trail. Jack tugged on the reins and urged his horse in the direction his spectral companion pointed. The dun set off at a quick trot through the wild grass. Satisfied, the spirit faded away. When Jack looked back at the spot where Andy had stood, he saw the reason for his brother's appearance. A prairie rattler, almost five feet long by Jack's estimation, curled along the trail in search of shade. Once they were far enough that Jack knew his horse wouldn't spook, he let the dun find its way back to the trail.

Three hours later, as the sun worked its way toward the horizon, Jack came upon the empty shell of an abandoned homestead. He appraised the structure. He felt played out and the way the duns' head hung, it needed a rest too. But the winds from a storm had torn the roof off the dwelling long ago and it would afford him little shelter. Jack decided to continue on. Andy peered out from an empty window frame. He gazed at something in the scrub brush. Jack saw that it was a hoe, left behind by the homesteaders when they had moved on.

From the past, the sound of metal striking flesh echoed in Jack's ears. He grabbed the saddle's horn for balance and shook his head as if to keep the memory at bay. It was no use.

"I'll race you, Jack!" Andy challenged and took off at a full sprint toward Rock Creek's main street. Jack let his younger brother get a good head start and then began to chase him. Twin plumes of dust marked the boys' progress, and then dissipated as they stood panting outside the post office. Their mother, referred to around town as 'the Widow Woman,' had sent the boys into Rock Creek from their farm to mail a letter. After their father's death, Mary had begun to correspond with kin back in Louisville. Unsure of how she would support herself and two boys here in the West, a move back to Kentucky seemed like the most practical option. It was Andy's job to mail the letter—a duty he attended to proudly. Jack was only along to supervise. Jack had no way of knowing he'd watch his little brother die that day.

Jack looked toward the shell of abandoned cabin, but Andy had faded away. Wearily, he picked up the reins. He was eager to leave the homestead—and the hoe—far behind. He wished he'd had to deal with the rattlesnake instead.

Three days passed as Jack slowly worked his way west.

The afternoon August sun found Jack approaching the foothills of the Black Hills. The imposing shape of Bear Butte loomed north of him; Fort Meade squatted to the south. Jack and the dun continued west and soon began to ascend the worn old mountains. The tall pines and spruce, spaced sporadically at first, began to thicken. Soon Jack was surrounded by trees. He felt peaceful, hidden. Only Andy interrupted Jack's solitude, occasionally appearing to point the way.

As they approached what the locals called Oyster Mountain, Andy appeared again, pointing at a small clear stream. The dun nickered happily at the prospect of water and rest and Jack contemplated making it their campsite for the night.

He removed the bridle from the dun and led it close to the stream. After he had tethered the horse securely in a location where the animal could drink and crop grass, he returned to the foot of the steep hill and squatted on his haunches. Jack gazed up at the rolling cloud banks and let his mind wander.

After mailing the letter, Andy and Jack descended the post office stairs and paused in the street. This rare trip to town afforded them a measure of freedom and after a brief conference, they decided on a detour to the general store for some hard candy before starting on their way back. As they passed the Overland stagecoach station, the door flew open abruptly and a tall man dressed in buckskin stepped out, slamming the door behind him. Raucous laughter came from within. The young man scowled and hurried into the street, long hair bouncing on his shoulders with each stride. He moved toward them, clenching his fists in anger. Both boys recognized James, the new stagecoach stable hand, as he approached. It was Andy, in the innocence of youth, who greeted him.

"Mornin', Mr. Duck Bill," he greeted the approaching figure in the silly voice that never failed to give Jack the fits. Jack began to laugh but stopped when he saw James' eyes blaze and his face flush crimson. James uttered a strangled cry of rage and ran up a side street. He jumped a fence and landed in someone's meager garden. The boys gaped first at him, then at each other.

"You made him go plum crazy!" Jack chided his dumbstruck younger brother. *"Why'd you go an' call him Duck Bill for?"*

"That's what Mr. McCanles and the fellers at the stage coach station call him." Andy defended himself. *"I was just bein' friendly."*

"I don't think he likes that nickname," Jack said. *"On account of his big nose."*

Andy's eyes widened. "Jack, he's comin' back!"

Something moved to Jack's left. Spooked, he made an awkward grab for his .45 caliber revolver. Andy's spectral form flickered before him. The spirit pointed toward the peak of the hill. Jack dutifully began to climb.

His boots slipped several times on the carpet of dry pine needles. The ascent was steeper than he had expected. The sun dipped below the horizon of the hills and as Jack climbed, the shadows lengthened and cool night air crept slyly across his face.

Near the top of Oyster Mountain, Jack approached an area where the pine needles and brush had been cleared away, exposing the dark earth. A sweat lodge constructed of thin tree branches and tanned buffalo hides sat in the center. The remains of a fire smoldered nearby and Jack saw one or two stones still heating amidst the embers. A lone Lakota stepped out of the sweat lodge and raised his hand in a somber greeting. "*How kola*," he said as Jack approached. "Hello, friend."

"*How kola*. Call me Jack."

"*Micaje Nape Sica.*"

Jack shrugged and shook his head. The other man gave it to him in English. "My name is Bad Hand."

"Are you alone here, or are there others?"

"I am *esnella*—a loner. I come to *Paha Sapa* because my heart cries for a vision."

Jack grunted noncommittally.

"*Wachin ksapa yo*," Bad Hand began. He paused and started again. "Listen to me." He gazed at the ground for a moment, carefully choosing his words. Then he resumed: "*Ki wanagi chikala*, the little spirit, came to me. My vision quest has already begun. He has asked me to share my *canupa*, my pipe, with you so that he may speak to you."

Bad Hand gestured for Jack to enter the sweat lodge. Jack wondered if it was Andy's ghost that had appeared before the Indian. Would he hear his brother's voice again after all these years?

"*Iyotaka*," Bad Hand said when they were inside, motioning Jack to sit down. A shallow pit in the center of the enclosure was filled with hot stones from the fire outside. The heat was so fierce that Jack stripped off his shirt as he waited for his eyes to adjust to the dark interior. He sat as far from the heated stones as he could and Bad Hand positioned himself opposite him, pouring water onto the stones. Steam billowed and Jack fought the feeling of claustrophobia that welled within him. After several minutes, Bad Hand repeated the procedure with the water. He next removed a small clay pipe from a leather pouch and filled it with tobacco. Bad Hand chanted a prayer and smoked. Jack waited, sweating and thinking about Andy. Finally Bad Hand passed the pipe across the stones and sat back.

"You are on *ki wanagi tacaku*, the spirit path," Bad Hand announced.

Jack held the pipe and raised his eyebrows skeptically. "Already?"

"You follow *ki wanagi chikalathe*, the little spirit, do you not?"

"What little spirit?"

"The spirit of your brother. He wishes to speak to you. Smoke to cleanse your mind and then be still."

Jack raised the pipe to his lips with trembling hands. He had grown used to seeing Andy, but was this his chance to *hear* him again? Jack inhaled and immediately coughed the smoke back out. His lungs felt scorched. He inhaled again and his lungs cooled. He felt a sense of peace wash over him. Bad Hand closed his eyes and began a chant. He seemed to Jack to be very far away. Jack's ears hummed.

Jack sat still and tried to relax, but felt as if he were melting in the heat. Even in almost complete darkness, shadows seemed to flit around the sweat lodge. The humming sound increased until it became unbearable. Jack closed his eyes and covered his ears against the growing roar.

"...aaaaaaaaaaaaaaahhhhhAAACK!"

Then silence.

"Jack!" The speaker repeated urgently.

Jack opened his eyes and looked at his brother Andy. They were sitting together in a grassy field. The warm sun shone down, all benevolence.

"Hi, Jack."

Tears welled in Jack's eyes. "I miss you, Andy," he croaked.

"I'm tired. I wanna go home."

"Are you leaving me?"

"You have to let me go first. You being sad is what is keeping me here."

"But—"

"Let me rest."

"How am I s'posed to forget you?"

"You don't need to forget me." Andy rippled like a heat mirage. "But there's poison in your heart and you need to get rid of it."

"I don't understand."

"You'll know when the time is right to balance the scales." The ghost held up his small transparent pink hands in a weighing gesture. "I have learned a lot, stuck between two worlds. I will help you."

"Andy, wait. I'm sorry." Jack broke off, not knowing how to apologize. Wanting to say he wished it was him that had died instead. The specter faded away and Jack felt a wave of nausea wash over him like rancid pond scum. He closed his eyes.

When he opened them again, he found himself back in the sweat lodge. Bad Hand chanted across from him. As Jack looked, the other man's eyelids fluttered and opened.

Bad Hand crawled from the sweat lodge into the cool night air. Jack put on his shirt and followed. The temperature change was so drastic that Jack briefly wondered if he'd been entranced for months and had awoken in the dead of winter. He shivered uncontrollably for several minutes while his companion panted nearby.

"That's something I never want to do again," Jack said finally. "That was bad medicine."

Bad Hand jerked his head up, insulted.

"*Canl Waka*, coward!" he spat. "You must accept the visions the spirit brings you."

"Well, then I reckon I'm supposed to kill a man," Jack said dryly.

Bad Hand regarded him closely. "That is your *sintkala waksu*, your spirit path?"

"Yes. My brother Andy told me. He died when we were kids. Said I would know when the time was right for vengeance."

"My path rapidly approaches the clearing. Soon my spirit will go to *Mahpiya*, to Paradise. It will be a hot day.

White men who are thirsty and tired of riding will run me down out of boredom and anger."

Jack didn't know the right words to say, so he kept silent.

"I have done no wrong," Bad Hand said. "My heart is good. Let *Wakan Tanka* come for me."

"I didn't have much schooling," Jack began, "but I know a raw deal when I see one. If what you say about bein' killed is true, then I'm sorry. I don't know why you were named Bad Hand, but pardner, it sounds like you been dealt one."

Jack fell asleep beneath the stars and woke beneath the sun. He sat up and rubbed his eyes. His muscles shrieked in protest and his joints felt stiff from spending the night sprawled on the earth. Bad Hand and the sweat lodge were gone. Jack wondered briefly if the other man had really been there at all.

He descended and drank deeply from the stream. Then he saddled up and rode deeper into the Black Hills. Jack urged his mount to the southwest, through Boulder Canyon. Andy appeared only when Jack began to wander off course. To the south, Granite Peak rose and sank behind them as they progressed. Jack rode to the top of a hill and was surprised by an expanse of meadow. The view, with Whitewood Peak to the north and Pillar Peak to the south, took his breath away. They rested briefly, Jack gnawing on jerked venison from his pack while the dun contentedly cropped the tall grass. He pondered his brother's words and slipped back again. Back to Kansas, and to Andy sprinting away in fear.

James thundered toward them, bright blue eyes blazing. The fringe of his buckskin bounced in time with his shoulder length hair. He was brandishing a garden hoe, stolen from a nearby garden. Its iron head gleamed in the sun. Andy turned and fled, but in his terror, he chose the path that eventually led home, rather than toward the potential protection of other townsfolk. Jack felt as if he were rooted to the earth. Where was everyone? Didn't anyone hear what was happening? It was only after James had bounded past him that fear for his brother outstripped his fear for himself. Jack spun and trailed after them.

In any race between a man in his early twenties and a nine-year-old boy, the boy always wins. This is because the older man allows the boy to win. This day, however, the man doing the running didn't care to observe that unspoken rule.

As Jack watched, helpless to intercede, James swung the hoe in a long arc. It connected with Andy's head and Jack heard the sound that he could never forget. Andy's small body sprawled to the ground in a cloud of dust.

It was afternoon again by the time Jack and his horse forded the stream in Spruce Gulch and began the slow ascent of another wooded hill. The wind and trees had conspired to play a trick on Jack and when he crested the next hill, he was met with a startling cacophony of sounds. The dun tossed its head with disapproval as Jack gaped at the settlement below. The bustling cavalcade of activity at the bottom of the hill nearly overwhelmed the senses.

Men shouted, laughed and called to one another. Grubby miners, cursing and spitting, led pack mules through the muddy, rutted streets. Dusty cowhands tilted their heads to look up at the kept women who flirted from the windows of their rooms. Some of the men turned away while others shuffled toward the brothel doors, looking both excited and foolish. A small group of men and women clotted one street corner as a tall man in black robes stood on a barrel and preached to his flock. Chinese men smiled obsequiously and pulled their carts, disappearing like ants into dark passageways. The tinkle of a piano came from one saloon. The bat-wing doors of another suddenly burst open and a barkeep and a sunburned cowboy tossed a dapper looking gambler into the dust. One or two respectable women of society ventured along the streets, while legitimate businessmen and bunko artists smoked cigars and eyed each other shrewdly. A group of Lakota Indians, in town for the day to trade, made an eye-catching spectacle of buckskin and feathers. Standing there in the midst of it all, looking up at Jack with supernatural clarity, stood Andy.

Jack sighed and started down the hill, following his spirit path straight into the heart of the mountain mining town.

After securing a stall for his horse in one of the outlying stables, Jack spent most of the hot July afternoon exploring the boom town. Andy had disappeared again as Jack was descending the hill so Jack wandered, doing his best not to idle anywhere too long. He didn't need anyone pegging him for a deadbeat. He browsed the mercantile, stopped for a questionable-tasting whiskey at one of the many saloons, and waved a good-natured dismissal toward a busty, toothless matron who was attempting to solicit clients from her windowsill.

Jack got a closer look at the tall bearded preacher as he exhorted his makeshift congregation. The preacher caught Jack's eyes and addressed him directly. "What brings you here, my son?"

"I want to help my brother find peace," Jack explained.

The preacher stretched out his arms and took in the crowd with a beatific gaze. "This man is here to help his brother," he cried. "That is what our Savior asks of all of us: to help one another!" Applause and scattered murmurs of approval came from the small crowd, and Jack took advantage of the moment to slip away down the street. Behind him Jack heard the preacher continue his sermon. "In Ecclesiastes, chapter four, Solomon writes..."

Jack kept wandering through the crowds searching for Andy, or for some sign of the man he needed to kill. He found neither. It was early in the evening now, with menacing dark thunderclouds rapidly rolling in from the north. A chilly gust of wind spat dust in his eyes. They watered as he hurried up the street. A rumble of thunder goaded several pedestrians into picking up their respective paces.

The sky overhead soon darkened and the first drops of rain splattered in the dust. The bare ground would soon become a quagmire and wagons jostled hurriedly up and down the streets. The horses pranced and reared nervously as the thunder increased in frequency and ferocity. People hurried indoors. The saloons and stores were suddenly filled to capacity. Miners scurried to their tent camps. The wind whipped at Jack as he sought shelter and he grabbed the front brim of his cowboy hat to stop it from blowing away.

Jack had a vague idea of heading for the nearest hotel when Andy appeared in the dimness of an adjacent alley. He stood with his hands behind his back and he seemed to gaze expectantly at his still-living brother. Jack turned and sprinted in Andy's direction.

Just ahead Jack saw wooden steps descending along side the building. Looking down, he saw the ghostly white face of his brother floating in the darkness below. The sky opened and rain began to drench the earth. Jack hurried down the stairs into the darkness below.

Andy was not waiting at the bottom of the steps, so Jack pushed open a red-painted wooden door. He stepped into a dark stone passageway, lit by lanterns hung on nails from the walls every twenty yards or so. Jack moved cautiously along the chilly passage. A rumbling sound came from somewhere in the darkness ahead. Suddenly the silhouette of a man emerged. As the figure approached, Jack was able to make him out more clearly. A small Chinese man pulled a wooden cart filled with carefully folded garments. The Chinese man showed no indication of slowing down as he approached and Jack was about to turn around and hurry back to the door when the little man executed a sharp turn and disappeared down a corridor Jack hadn't noticed. The rumble of the cart's wheels faded away and Jack heard only the gentle hiss of the oil lamps and the distant rumble of thunder.

Why had Andy guided him here? Just to get him out of the rain? Jack knew there had to be more to it than that. As quietly as he could, he stepped toward the tunnel the Chinese launderer had taken. Unconsciously holding his breath, he peered cautiously around the corner.

"Why you make so much noise?" a sharp voice complained from behind him and Jack jolted in surprise. He spun around and saw a wizened old Chinese man standing in the opposite passageway. The elderly man wore a shimmery black jacket embroidered with white thread. His dark eyes seemed to flicker in the gas light and a long white mustache hung like cobwebs from both sides of his thin mouth.

"I am Shen Liu. You are late," he continued curtly, like a schoolmarm admonishing a tardy student. "Come."

The Chinese man turned and moved down a passage so small that Jack had to stoop in order to enter. Jack followed the old man down the pitch-black tunnel. His guide told him when to turn left or right or when there was a step up or down. After a period of prolonged silence, Jack began to feel claustrophobic.

"Where are you taking me?" Jack muttered. "I'm a cowpuncher, not a miner searching for the mother lode."

Suddenly a hand grabbed the back of Jack's collar and hauled him backwards into a dimly lit den. Jack spun around and reached for his revolver but was shocked to find his holster empty. On the verge of panic, Jack realized it was Shen Liu standing in front of him.

"You very slow," the Chinese man said. He handed back the gun. Jack took it, stupefied. The old man gestured toward a luxuriant rug. "Sit."

Jack eased himself to the floor and sat cross-legged before a wooden tray. The tray itself was elaborately decorated with ivory inlays and pearlescent seashells. Atop the wooden tray were a variety of items including two smaller metal trays; a tiny oil lamp; a pipe with a bamboo stem; and a blue and white porcelain bowl. The old man sat down across from Jack.

"Your brother came to me yesterday as I smoked," Shen Liu said as he trimmed the wick on the little oil lamp. "His round white face and black eyes nearly scared the life from me."

"At least there's still some life left in you to scare," Jack remarked.

The old man filled a pipe using something that looked to Jack like a skeleton key with a tiny spoon at one end.

"An-dee is his name?"

Jack nodded.

"He speak of the sorrow you and he share." Shen Liu held the pipe over the flame burning in the lamp. "He ask me to help you."

The old man raised his pipe to his lips and inhaled deeply. He closed his eyes and his shoulders sank as he relaxed.

"We build tunnels for laundry, but have many secret places as well." The old man arched an eyebrow slyly. Jack glanced around the dimly lit alcove.

"Bill, ready to pay," Shen Liu continued. Jack concentrated, trying to follow the old man's words. *What had he said? A bill needed to be paid?*

Shen Liu held the pipe out to Jack. He took it and tentatively inhaled. Rather than making him cough, the smoke was thick and sweet. It felt like molasses coating his lungs. Jack felt the tension flow from his body.

Shen Liu held the pipe over the flame. Then he returned it to Jack who put the small pipe to his lips and inhaled again. The room tilted sharply and Jack toppled onto the rug, his limbs felt simultaneously weightless and unbearably heavy. He thought he heard Andy singing a song they had learned as children. Jack was dimly aware of the old Chinese man retiring to a corner of the room. The opium was a shock to Jack's system. He thought he saw someone else in the room but the presence always flitted just out of his field of vision.

"Aces and eights are the most important cards in a deck." Andy's voice seemed to come from nowhere and everywhere. "I also like the number ten."

Jack scarcely dared to breathe as he concentrated on his dead brother's child-like ramblings.

"One shot."

The sound of flies buzzing around his ears woke him and Jack sat up, groggily rubbing his eyes. The bedsprings creaked in protest as he rolled over and swung his legs onto the floor. Jack noticed a water pitcher and a glass on a battered dresser. He walked over, ignored the glass and gratefully gulped the liquid straight from the pitcher. Jack shook his head, trying to clear it. Scattered images of the previous night paraded through his memory: the Chinese laundry tunnels, Shen Liu, the opium pipe and Andy's cryptic words.

Jack screamed his brother's name as he ran to where Andy lay. He slid to the ground and gathered his brother in his arms. James dropped the hoe absently, his bright blue eyes showing a mixture of fear and gratification. Jack rocked Andy in his arms. He palmed a trickle of blood from his brother's cheek and began to sob. He knew he was too old to cry, but this was different. He cried for his brother, lying so still. He cried when he thought about breaking the news to their mother. And he cried because he had no father to break the news to.

Jack gulped the rest of the water. His hand trembled so violently that he dribbled most of what was left down the front of his shirt. Then Jack grabbed his boots from their place beside the bed and pulled them on. He buckled on his holster, grabbed his hat and descended the stairs. Jack stopped at the desk to inquire about payment. The desk clerk, a tall man with spectacles and carefully oiled and combed hair, informed Jack that 'an old Chinaman' had brought him in and paid for the room the night before. The clerk volunteered to hold the room if Jack intended to return.

"Much obliged," Jack told the clerk. He left the lobby and stepped into the bright noonday sun. Jack rambled up and down the streets of the bustling town, casually taking in the sights, but always on the lookout for Andy or the man he needed to find. About mid-afternoon, Jack stepped into a restaurant for a bite to eat. He ordered liver and onions and Arbuckle's coffee. As Jack paid he realized he was dangerously low on funds. He'd have to find work, and soon. Maybe tonight he could win a few hands of poker to get him by for a few more days.

On his way out, Jack asked the man running the place where the best spots for poker were. "Every saloon in town has games running every night," the ruddy-faced man said, scratching at his scalp. "Seems like a lot of the high rollers make an appearance over at the No. 10."

Jack raised his eyebrows. "Number ten?"

"Sure. Nuttal and Mann's Saloon No. 10."

Jack headed outside thinking that he might try his hand against a few of these so-called 'high rollers'. He stepped into the street and stopped short.

Andy had said something about the number ten. Jack's eyes narrowed and he turned and marched purposefully down Main Street.

Jack almost missed his intended destination. The sign hanging from the saloon was small and unassuming. As Jack approached, a grubby miner burst through a set of bat-wing doors and stuck a filthy finger in Jack's face. He seemed about to speak, but before he could, a brawny barkeep grabbed the miner by the collar and tossed him into the dirt.

"Don't mind him; he's full as a tick," the barkeep said to Jack.

"I see that."

"Name's Harry Young," the barkeep said as he opened one of the doors to go back inside. "I run a tight ship here at the No. 10."

His stomach tightening in a way he did not quite understand, Jack followed the man inside.

A few hours later Jack found himself gazing at his brother's killer.

The man had arrived at the No. 10 amidst the admiring looks of nearly everyone in and around the bar. James was a hard man to miss, standing several inches above most others. His long wavy hair spilled onto a buckskin fringed coat and a scraggly handlebar mustache diminished the appearance of his protruding nose and petulant lips.

Someone bought James a drink. He downed it in a gulp and stationed himself near one of the tables. Sensing that the tall man wanted in, one of the players threw in his hand and vacated his chair. Jack was surprised when Andy appeared in the empty seat. Yet no one else noticed. Andy stared directly at Jack, his eyes dull and hollow. Then the big gambler dropped into the chair and obliterated the apparition.

The symbolism was not lost on Jack, who seethed as the cards flew.

Andy's killer had achieved a great deal of notoriety in recent years. Everyone referred to the tall man not as James, but a different name. Jack didn't know if it was a nickname or an alias. He wondered if James had changed his name after fleeing Rock Creek. Jack's blood ran cold as he watched the tall man handle his cards.

Jack hovered, tossing back occasional whiskey shots and steeling his nerve. When another of the players dropped out, Jack stepped forward and took his place.

"Reckon I know you," Jack addressed Andy's killer as the cards were dealt.

"Reckon everybody does," the tall man shot back and the room erupted in laughter. Both men eyed their cards. Jack kept a pair of tens and discarded his three undesirables. His new cards amounted to nothing and he folded. The man to Jack's left discarded a pair of cards and the dealer, sitting to Jack's right, tossed him two more.

"Mebbe you remember me from Rock Creek, Kansas," Jack pressed.

James looked up.

Jack expected to see the shock of recognition in the other man's eyes. Successful gambler that he was, however, James' facial features and body language betrayed no reaction.

"Never been there," he said.

Without breaking eye contact, James tossed one card and received another. He tossed a coin into the pot. The dealer stayed and tossed in his coin. The player to Jack's left folded.

James raised. The dealer called.

"Straight," James said, fanning his cards.

"Beats my two pair," the dealer admitted, and James swept up the pot.

So went the evening and much of the night. The tall man continued playing to the gallery, cracking jokes and accepting free drinks. Jack won a few small pots but kept playing and soon found he was dead broke. He pushed back his chair and stood, fuming. Feeling desperate, but not knowing what to do, he headed for the bat-wing doors. He had to get outside, gather his wits...

Andy lay in Jack's arms, lifeless as a log.

Jack shot beseeching looks in every direction. The only living person he saw was James shuffling back towards town. Seized by a sudden fury, Jack screamed.

"I'll kill you when I grow up! If I ever see you again I will KILL YOU!"

James did not turn around. Instead, he returned to town, mounted the first horse he found and immediately fled Kansas.

"Hey, puncher!"

Jack stopped short. The voice belonged to James.

"I feel awful about fleecing you," the gambler said, amid snickers from several onlookers. "Let me pay for dinner tonight and breakfast tomorrow." James tossed a couple coins in Jack's direction.

Reflexively, Jack caught the arcing coins.

"I'll be right here tomorrow night," James said, still looking at Jack. Now his eyes seemed to burn with secret meaning. "If you decide to settle accounts."

Jeering laughter chased Jack out into the darkness. His blood pounded in his temples as he staggered through the humid night air. He hurried across the still-muddy street and ducked into the shadows between two buildings.

Jack suddenly realized that James, unlike the others, hadn't been laughing. He stood pondering this. Perhaps Jack wasn't the only tortured soul haunted by the past. He tried to imagine James tossing and turning through sleepless nights. He wondered if the other man ever saw Andy's face in nightmares or during waking hours.

Jack found his way back to the same hotel and gave the desk clerk the coins.

He clutched at the banister as he ascended the stairs, his brain swimming with unanswered questions. Inside the room, Jack kicked off his boots, took off his gun belt and collapsed onto the mattress.

It seemed as if the gambler's voice echoed in Jack's ears all night long. *"I'll be right here tomorrow night if you decide to settle accounts."*

Jack's mouth was dry as he slipped into the Saloon No. 10 the next night. He moved down the bar, stopping a few steps away from a table of poker players. He stood directly behind the man who had killed his brother. Several others were gathered around the table, taking a look at the hands that were dealt.

James raised his cards and Jack saw that the top one was a jack. Jack realized the face on the card bore an eerie resemblance to his own image. Then he noticed that the other cards in James' hand were all aces and eights. Andy's words came back to Jack with chilling clarity.

James sat very still, doing nothing with his cards, and Jack realized the big man was waiting for him. *Waiting for me to settle accounts. Balance the scales.* Andy flickered in and out of view beside the table. His eyes gazed longingly upward at something that Jack could not see.

Knowing the time was right Jack raised his Colt .45 and aimed the barrel directly at James Butler Hickok's back. Before anyone could react, Jack McCall pulled the trigger and finally set his brother's spirit free.

CARRYING ON

Once the enormity of our situation became apparent, half the population carried on like it was the end of the world. The other half carried on *despite* it being the end of the world.

A day and a half ago various news sources reported that a group of astronomers believed an asteroid roughly a mile wide would smash into Canada within the next forty-eight hours but no one paid much attention. I half-listened to the newscaster on television say something about a collision with space junk and an altered trajectory. The asteroid even had a name that astronomers had given it, but it was all numbers and letters, and I didn't even try to remember it. The newscaster said the asteroid was travelling at 30,000 mph. My wife made a joke about the highway patrol using a radar gun to clock its speed and we had a chuckle over that.

I wasn't scared, just mildly curious. That night, before bed, I looked for the story online. The reports conflicted. Some of the articles I glanced at even mocked the astronomers, saying their warnings of "an impact-caused extinction event" were merely paranoia. So I forgot about it. So did most of the world.

Twenty four hours later, though, when it was revealed that our new president and most of the other NATO-affiliated world leaders had ensconced themselves in secret underground bunkers, the red flags finally went up.

A cascade of violence and looting came, of course. It was counterbalanced by a spike in prayer groups and packed churches. Scientists worked round-the-clock toward a viable solution without apparent success.

BEDTIME STORIES FOR CARRION BEETLES

A few of my office coworkers didn't come in at all that morning and when Roger, our division's supervisor, announced that staying was optional, most staffers bolted for the doors, Roger among them. Others stayed, apparently not knowing what else to do. There is comfort in routine. No one can dispute that. Perhaps focusing on menial tasks was easier than facing the truth.

I called my wife's cell. Voice mail picked up and I was forced to leave a message. I told her that I loved her and asked her not to worry. I wondered if she'd ever hear my words.

From two cubicles over, I heard Meredith's hysterical sobs. I tried calling my daughter in St. Paul but no one answered there either. As I counted the rings, Ted and Will's heated discussion of pending events escalated from mouths to fists.

I decided I wasn't content to sit in my cubicle and wait for the end to come. I pulled open the bottom desk drawer and rummaged around until I found the objects that would take me to the end of my existence. The smaller items inside slid and clicked against one another as I placed the paperboard box on my desk.

Hairy Harry looked shell-shocked.

I'd never taken the time to learn his real name. Hairy Harry just sounded right for the scraggly-haired, wild-eyed man invariably stationed on the corner of Lexington and 44th. I had passed him every morning for three years as I walked between the subway station and the office. Both Harry and his carefully lettered cardboard sign unwaveringly proclaimed: *"Repent! The end is near!"*

Today the sign hung limply from one grimy hand and Harry was silent.

I walked up and spoke to him for the first time. "You were right."

Harry focused watery eyes on me and shook his head in disbelief. "Never thought I'd live to see the day..."

The sound of sirens grew and then faded in the distance. Somewhere a car alarm wailed. People hurried up and down the sidewalks, arguing, weeping, and shouting frantically into cell phones. You could almost close your eyes and pretend it was just another day in the big city. *Almost.*

A breathtaking orange light colored the normally blue sky. The view inspired in me a deep feeling of dread. It looked so *wrong*. The fingernail moon looked like the hand of God directing celestial traffic saying: *"Hit right here."*

I turned back to my companion and held up the box I'd taken from my desk drawer. He broke into a bittersweet smile when he saw what it contained. Harry shuffled a few yards into the cool mouth of an alley and I followed. We sat facing each other, cross-legged on the dirty asphalt. Harry placed his cardboard sign on our laps and I unloaded the contents of the box in the center.

Over Harry's shoulder I saw a speeding motorist run down an elderly woman trying to cross the street. The thump and boom of explosions emanated from the river's edge. My hand shook as I continued placing the objects from the box in their allotted spaces, following time-honored tradition.

"You want to go first?" I asked when everything was prepared. The sky was a bright orange now. It hurt my eyes.

"Sure." Hairy Harry slid one of the black checkers forward to a new space.

I moved one of the red checkers.

We carried on until the end of the world.

SWOLLEN TICK

Part I
Feast

With preternatural clarity, Melvin listened to the bitter January wind howling between the buildings, the landlord wheezing, a cell phone's chirp and canned sitcom laughter. He also heard—and felt—his stomach rumbling. Melvin waited for the landlord to select the correct key from the large ring and then they were inside the small apartment. The landlord had introduced himself as Cal Rogers. He was a short bald man with a bristly mustache and ruddy complexion. Melvin's impression of the man was that he was blissfully unaware of the unhappiness and squalor which surrounded him.

"She's small but clean," Rogers said, beaming. He pulled open the curtains in an attempt to let in more light, but the sun had already sunk below the skyscrapers opposite the apartment building.

"Nice view of the city," the landlord said. He motioned outside with one arm like a game show hostess marveling over a prize-packed showcase.

Melvin glanced out and grunted noncommittally.

"Kitchen's over here." Rogers droned on. Melvin nodded intermittently. He listened and waited for something *more*.

The landlord scurried up the short hallway. "Come check out the bed and bath."

The bedroom was only slightly larger than most walk-in closets. Dead flies lay in drifts on the sill between the glass pane and the screen. A variety of stains broke up the monotony of the beige carpet. The bathroom fixtures looked like they should have been replaced decades ago. Overall, the aesthetics of the little apartment left much to be desired.

The couple living next door had begun to argue, hurling angry insults at each other with apparent relish. The landlord droned on, unconsciously raising his voice to drown out the bickering tenants.

Melvin raised a hand to silence Rogers. He smiled reassuringly at the little man.

"It's perfect," Melvin said. He swallowed the saliva which had suddenly filled his mouth. "I'll take it."

#

Melvin stretched languidly on the couch. His neighbors, the Coughlins, were at it again. Melvin closed his eyes and concentrated on their words to see what they were fighting about this time.

"People do it all the time, fer crissakes!" Barry Coughlin complained. His booming, gravelly voice perfectly matched the oversize frame of an aging former jock.

"Well, I don't!" retorted his wife Shirley. She was a diminutive woman with dishwater blond hair and gray-green eyes. "And I will not. If that's something you think you need, then you can just pack your suitcase right now!"

"Everything I do for you and you can't even—"

"If you're going to keep talking about it, I'm leaving!"

"Fine, go!"

A door slammed then, but Melvin knew the woman had not gone. Instead, she was sulking in the bedroom. Melvin heard Barry mumbling angrily. He was probably grabbing himself a beer from their refrigerator. Then he'd sit and seethe resentfully in front of the television for a few hours.

Melvin yawned and sat up. He'd had enough. His thoughts turned to his own household. Melvin stood and padded into the kitchen. Today he had set aside some time to make up a new grocery list. He'd been living here a month now and needed to restock some necessities.

#

Customers raced their carts up and down the supermarket aisles like mice in a maze. Melvin sampled their negative emotions the way other customers sometimes helped themselves to the food on display. But instead of popping a grape into his mouth in one aisle and sneaking a few peanuts in another, Melvin siphoned off a bit of the anger that came from each harried mother who admonished a squalling child. In the cereal aisle an exasperated woman struggled to mentally add up her purchases and Melvin paused for a taste of her frustration. Two aisles further, a man frantically tried to remember what his domineering wife had sent him out to buy. A grocery store employee grumbled as he mopped up the melting slush near the entrance. Melvin wheeled his cart up and down the aisles, occasionally selecting an item, occasionally absorbing a negative emotion.

"Hey man, can you help me out?"

Melvin was startled from his reverie by a younger man in a poncho. His hair hung in blond dreadlocks and the acrid odor of patchouli oil assaulted Melvin's nose.

"What is it?" he asked, trying not to breathe.

"Dude, I have no idea what to do," the younger man said with emphasized gravity. "Should I get ketchup...or catsup?" He held up two identical looking plastic bottles and Melvin peered at first one, then the other.

Melvin furrowed his brow in concentration then looked again into the other man's bloodshot eyes. "I'm afraid I don't know which to recommend. Perhaps someone who works here can help."

"Forget it, dude," the dreadlocked man snorted. "That was s'posed to be a joke!" He spun on his sandaled heel and shuffled away, muttering. Melvin absorbed some of the other man's annoyance, though he didn't understand what he'd done to cause it.

The checkout lanes were a logjam of carts and customers. Everyone seemed eager to go home. Melvin stood patiently in line, soaking it all in. Around him scanners beeped, registers spit out receipts and cashiers shook open plastic sacks. Just for fun, Melvin slipped a jar of caviar into the cart of the woman ahead of him when she wasn't looking. He had to stifle a chuckle of satisfaction as the woman and the cashier bickered over the unexpected extra cost.

Melvin sighed with contentment as he loaded his purchases into the back seat. He always found trips to the grocery store rewarding. He'd picked up some hand soap, deodorant, hair gel, foot powder and a small potted plant for the window sill. Melvin, as usual, did not buy any food.

#

Upon returning to his apartment, he could hear the couple arguing again. This time Barry was taking Shirley to task for burning the meatloaf. Melvin unscrewed the cap from the milk jug and poured about a cup's worth down the drain. Shirley called her husband a depraved dimwit. Barry retorted by accusing his wife of proving again that she was a spiteful prude. A dish crashed and shattered against the common wall between the dwellings. The sound of angry footsteps and slamming doors came from next door. All was finally quiet next door.

Melvin then shuffled into the living room and sank down onto the couch, utterly content. He read for a while then dozed.

Things went on like this for five blissful weeks. Melvin put on so much weight, some nights he had to go to bed wearing earplugs.

Part II
Famine

Melvin awoke to what felt like a horde of fire ants seething inside his belly. The blankets on the bed felt as heavy as a coffin lid. He grimaced and struggled to untangle himself from the sweat-soaked sheets. He hadn't felt well and had retired early the night before. Melvin wondered how much time had passed since he had gone to sleep. Had it really only been the previous night? His stomach twisted angrily as if he hadn't eaten in days.

Knowing that trying to go back to sleep would not only be futile but would also lead to an escalation of his pain, Melvin crawled from the bed and struggled into his clothes. He had to get out of his building, go somewhere public.

Melvin dressed and hurried down the stairs, holding onto the dirty railing for balance. He staggered out onto the street and joined the throng of pedestrians on the sidewalk. After a few minutes Melvin began to feel a little better, so he let himself wander. He thought a small pub might make for a good meal, but the patrons were all in relatively good spirits and he found little to assuage his pangs of hunger.

Retail stores began to dwindle as he made his way up the street, and Melvin stopped to survey the businesses on the next block. He saw signs for a tax preparation service, a chiropractor's office and a walk-in clinic.

Following his intuition, Melvin crossed the street and entered the clinic's waiting room. He picked up a celebrity gossip magazine that was several weeks old and gingerly slid into a chair in one corner as inconspicuously as he could manage. A pretty brunette woman sat and worried about her young daughter's fever. Another woman, middle-aged and slightly overweight, wondered if the lump she had felt was really breast cancer. A sweating man in a clerical collar sat alone, silently wondering if his kidney stones were a test from God. Melvin soaked it all in.

When he left the clinic thirty minutes later, his hunger was sated.

But Melvin knew the satisfaction was only temporary. Something had gone wrong during the last week. Something had changed the dynamics of the Coughlins' relationship. His neighbors never fought or argued anymore. Melvin was still eating, but not nearly enough. He found that he could snack on the negative emotions of his coworkers and others he encountered in day-to-day life, but the constant bickering of his neighbors was the meat and potatoes of his existence. At least it *had been*. Melvin mused on this as he strode back to his apartment.

"Hello, neighbor!" boomed a jovial voice. Melvin turned to see Barry Coughlin approaching.

"Hello to you," Melvin replied. He held the door open for his neighbor and noticed that the man was carrying a bouquet of roses. "What's the occasion?"

"Valentine's Day," Barry replied. Exuberance tempered by a twinge of self-consciousness intermingled on his face. The exuberance left an unpleasant taste in Melvin's mouth.

"Normally I wouldn't have gotten flowers, but Shirley and I started going to marriage counseling."

Melvin's heart sank. His stomach gurgled and he gazed bleakly at his neighbor.

"The marriage has always been a little rocky," Barry admitted, as if Melvin wasn't already aware. "Then one day, during one of our spats, Shirley says 'I need a translator when I talk to you.' It was just an offhand comment but it was like a light went on in my head, y'know?"

Melvin managed a weak nod, not liking where the monologue was heading.

"So that's what we did," Barry said. "We looked up 'marital counseling' in the phone book and picked out a name with an office near here. Dan Montgomery is the guy's name. It's been amazing; we're like a completely different couple. This Valentine's Day marks a new beginning for us."

"So glad to hear it," Melvin croaked weakly. He contorted his face into what he hoped passed as a smile. Melvin felt like he had just ingested pink fiberglass insulation, mistaking it for cotton candy. He plodded up the stairs behind his high-spirited neighbor.

#

Melvin withered. Neither his coworkers nor any of his other neighbors provided enough sustenance. He needed more pain, anger, sorrow. Taking a walk outside or going for a drive through town helped take the edge off his hunger pangs, but Melvin knew he could not survive on crumbs thrown from strangers. The dramatic programs on television sounded right, but held no nutritional content. He tossed restlessly on his couch, turning the problem over in his mind. He knew he had to take drastic measures. Starvation was an agonizing way to go.

Once in a while, Melvin would discover that one of his brothers or sisters had perished. 'Spontaneous combustion', the papers invariably called it. Sometimes the paper would print a grainy photograph showing the charred smear of ash on an otherwise untouched recliner or bed. Their insensitivity always broke his heart.

He floundered from his uneasy perch on the couch as if prolonged contact with the article of furniture would precipitate combustion. He had to get the Coughlins fighting again; it was as simple as that. He was not strong enough to hunt for another apartment in his present condition.

Melvin hugged himself and tottered across his living room floor as he pondered his problem. He briefly considered standing vigil at his peephole until either Barry or Shirley left their apartment. He'd wait until they reached the top of the stairs and then spring from his own dwelling to send his victim hurtling down the stairs. Then he could feast on the sorrow of the survivor.

No. Melvin questioned his ability to actually follow through with such an endeavor, and the results were too hard to predict. Suppose someone saw him do it? Or what if the surviving half of the couple handled grief better than Melvin had anticipated? What if they simply moved away after the tragedy and were replaced by someone happier? What if the person he pushed survived and told police what had happened? There were too many questions; too many variables that could go wrong.

Finally, an idea presented itself and he grinned with relief and excitement. He hurried into the kitchen. Melvin tore a page from the tablet he kept there and carefully began to write. After several minutes, Melvin held the page up and reread what he hoped would be his salvation.

Dearest Shirley,

You're right. That dumb lummox husband of yours has no idea what's really going on. When we conduct our sessions, it's all I can do not to burst out laughing. If he knew half the things you and I have done in that office and on my desk I believe his head would explode! Just keep smiling and acting like you are happy with him. And if he starts to get angry or suspicious, just accuse him of sabotaging the marriage with unfounded jealousy. It works every time! Can't wait to see you again!

Lustfully yours, Dan.

Melvin nodded with satisfaction. He found a blank envelope and folded the note carefully inside. Now all he had to do was fight through the encroaching pain and find the patience to wait for morning.

Without bothering to undress, Melvin collapsed onto his bed, where he immediately slipped into unconsciousness.

Part III
The Cup Runneth Over

Melvin awoke curled up like a dead insect in the center of his bed. The cramps in his stomach kept his knees stapled to his chin. He felt more feverish than ever.

Melvin strained his ears. The clock on his nightstand dominated the soundscape; each tick seeming to bring Melvin closer to his impending deliverance. The fuzzy gray light of dawn peeked shyly in through his windows. Then, from far below, Melvin heard a dog bark. Soon a garbage truck rumbled through the alley. Melvin heard the engine roar as its driver accelerated across the main street, earning an angry honk from another early morning motorist who had apparently been cut off. Melvin flexed his fingers experimentally and found that though his muscles burned, he still had at least some reserve strength left within him. He listened intently. The Coughlins would be waking soon. Shirley would be up first, making breakfast for the two of them, then showering and dressing for work while her husband ate. Melvin knew both Barry and Shirley started work at the same time, but Barry's place of work was the closer of the two. Shirley had to catch a cross-town bus to get to the dentist's office where she worked as a receptionist, so she was always first out of the apartment. That would work to Melvin's advantage. He closed his eyes and tried to relax, waiting for the alarm next door to sound.

He dozed again then awoke to the sound of the Coughlins' alarm clock. He drifted in and out of consciousness, mentally noting the passing of time in correlation with the sounds he heard. Murmurs passed between the man and his wife, the sound of water running, doors opening and closing. The sun proudly threw golden rays in through Melvin's window around the time he finally heard Shirley's heels clip-clop past his door and diminish down the stairs. He stretched cautiously and rolled from his bed. Melvin retrieved the letter and held it in trembling hands. He nervously began to lick his lips but his tongue was like sandpaper and he stopped short. In his present condition, licking his lips would be like dragging a match across a strike plate. He'd be the next tabloid headline and grainy front page photo if he wasn't extremely careful.

Melvin waited a few more minutes, then gingerly left his apartment and rapped gently on the Coughlins' door. He counted to twenty and then knocked again. Barry's heavy step approached and the door opened a crack. Melvin smiled apologetically and the bigger man swung the door open wide upon seeing who it was.

"Morning, neighbor," Barry greeted him.

"Good morning," Melvin replied. "Sorry to bother you so early, but I was wondering if Shirley was available."

Coughlin's eyebrows elevated slightly. "Shirley?"

"Yes." Melvin held up the letter he had inscribed the night before, ensconced within its envelope, ready to detonate like a bomb. Melvin's mouth watered at the thought of the impending fallout.

"What's that?" Barry inquired.

"I'm not sure," Melvin replied. "I saw Shirley early this morning on the stairs. After she passed, I noticed she'd dropped this. Being a good neighbor, I thought I'd better return it." He offered the envelope to the bigger man, who took it with furrowed brows.

"Thanks," Barry offered neutrally. Melvin could almost see the questions already floating in the bigger man's eyes.

"Don't mention it. Have a nice day." Melvin fought the urge to scamper back to his own apartment and instead casually sauntered down the hall. He heard Coughlin close his door and hazarded a glance back. Any second now, he thought.

Melvin had just closed his own door and was leaning with his back against it when the first wave hit him. It was an effervescent influx of warmth and kinetic energy that refreshed and satisfied immediately. Melvin heard his neighbor curse bitterly and then came another nourishing wave. Barry Coughlin raged and sobbed and Melvin feasted on his pain.

#

Neither man went to work that day.

Melvin puttered around his apartment for the rest of the morning. As afternoon arrived and the sun began its gentle descent, Melvin found himself continually distracted by the thought of Shirley's impending arrival. It was all he could do not to rub his hands together with glee at the banquet that he had laid out for himself. Melvin had felt the cold breath of Death on his neck, and like the old sailors of legend who guarded against starvation by hoarding biscuits in their mattresses, Melvin would ingest as much nourishment as his body could possibly take. Who knew when an opportunity like this would present itself again?

At last Melvin's ears picked up the sound of Shirley's heels clicking as she ascended the stairs. Melvin's pulse quickened. He had removed his earplugs about an hour earlier and had heard only ominous silence through the wall since. That was about to change. Melvin heard keys jingling and stealthily approached the shared wall between his apartment and the Coughlins'. He placed his palms against the cool plaster. A symbolic move, but at that moment it felt right.

"Honey?" It was Shirley's voice.

"Your lover boy left you a note, you two-faced bitch."

Barry's growled proclamation gave Melvin chills of pleasure. He felt another energetic surge.

"Lover boy?" Shirley's voice was still flat with incomprehension.

"That friggin' counselor you been so hot to make sure we visit all the time. Now I know why."

"Dan Montgomery? Barry, what are you talking about? I am not attracted to him at all."

"Bullshit! You've been playing me for a fool, Shirley. Not anymore."

Shirley apparently realized the stakes were higher than she'd first imagined. Her voice rose up an octave as she fought against her rising panic. "Barry, please! Let's talk this over like adults before you sabotage our marriage with your unfounded jealousy."

Melvin barely stifled a shriek of surprised delight. He gained twenty pounds from the influx of rage that erupted from Barry at those unfortunately-chosen words. The sacs attached to his eardrums converted the negative emotions into a physical residue and Melvin's circulatory system kicked in to overdrive, trying to keep up with and distribute the influx of nourishment.

The sound of Barry's pounding footsteps preceded a muffled cry and a tremendous crashing sound. Melvin reeled away from the wall and staggered toward his couch. He heard the meaty sound of fists connecting with flesh. Melvin collapsed onto the couch, but then rolled helplessly onto the floor with a groan of pleasure. The sounds of violence continued for nearly a minute.

Melvin was about to stick chubby fingers into his ears when the noises stopped. He lay panting on the floor, awash with a feeling not dissimilar to post-coital afterglow. Melvin had just experienced an orgasmic feast of the senses. He felt weak and clumsy, like an inebriated stranger had taken control of body.

The silence next door proved to be short lived. Barry Coughlin's regret and repentance welled up and spilled out of him in anguished sobs. Melvin wrinkled his nose, having no taste for the dessert that was being offered. He tried to cover his ears and found he'd grown so morbidly obese that he could no longer fit his fingers into his ears.

Then he heard the crash of breaking glass and the diminishing shriek as Barry committed his final act of contrition. Melvin felt an emotion as near to panic as fog is to rain. His face contorted into a fearful leer of regret. As his weight ballooned, Melvin wondered if he'd actually explode as a result of his gluttony.

#

Instead of exploding, Melvin slept through much of what followed; from the cacophony of sirens heralding the arrival of emergency vehicles on the street below to the later discovery of the brutality committed within the Coughlins' apartment. It was late the next afternoon before Melvin fully revived. He experimentally stretched his limbs and yawned contentedly.

The sudden and extreme weight gain would be virtually impossible to explain to his coworkers. Melvin decided he would phone in his resignation. He had enough money saved to tide him over for a while. He decided he would mail Rogers the monthly rent check.

The police would undoubtedly stop by to take a statement from him. Melvin hadn't answered their knocks the previous afternoon and he knew they'd return. He just had to be honest—at least up to a point. Melvin would simply tell them what he had heard. And since none of the officers knew him, there would be no particular notice taken of his extraordinary weight gain.

Melvin smiled. He estimated that he might not have to feed again for three, maybe four months. He grunted with effort and forced his rotund frame into a sitting position. Then he used the couch to aid him in gaining his feet. The floorboards creaked beneath his weight as he waddled to the kitchen. He removed a tablet and pencil from a drawer and set them on the immaculately clean counter.

BEDTIME STORIES FOR CARRION BEETLES

In a week or two, when he would be able to move with more ease, he'd go on a shopping excursion. Perhaps he'd pick up some mouthwash this time. And shampoo. But no food would be necessary; he'd already devoured plenty.

TOMORROW'S HEADLINE

Michelle Watkins thought her day couldn't get any worse. She was wrong.

She'd just dropped off the dry cleaning when the telltale swirling orbs of white light began to encroach on her vision. Michelle knew a migraine was rapidly approaching. She groaned inwardly and gripped the wheel.

From the back seat Casey, his voice dripping with the sweet purity of youth, sang: "Robot pa-rade, robot pa-rade..."

"Casey, honey," Michelle had to raise her voice to be heard. "Mommy is getting a headache. Can you please stop singing?"

Casey caught her eye in the rear view mirror and stopped singing. He started kicking the back of her seat instead.

Michelle sighed and yanked the Impala's shifter into reverse. On the street behind her, the driver of a late model Chevy pickup leaned on his horn. Michelle winced as the sound grated her ears. "Go ahead then," she said aloud as if the pickup's driver could actually hear her, "Save ten seconds."

The pickup roared up the street and Michelle looked out the rear window before cautiously backing up again. Casey, momentarily distracted by the honking truck, mercifully forgot about kicking her seat. Michelle decided to detour to the drug store before heading home. It was only four blocks from the dry cleaners and then eight or nine blocks back home. She could turn on cartoons for Casey and then hide from the pain in the comforting confines of her darkened bedroom.

At the stoplight Casey started kicking her seat again.

"Casey, quit!" This triggered the song again. Michelle rubbed her eyes in a fruitless attempt at clearing her vision. Her vision swirled in a bluish haze. Nausea would be setting in soon, then the crippling pain.

The light turned green and Michelle was eager to push down on the gas but a chubby kid lugging what appeared to be a trombone case hadn't made it across the street yet. She ground her teeth with frustration until the kid reached the curb then pressed down on the accelerator.

Michelle sped the two remaining blocks and eased the Impala into the first empty parking spot she found. She closed her eyes and massaged the back of her neck in a fruitless attempt at relieving her discomfort. Michelle inhaled deeply, held it, and slowly exhaled. She repeated this exercise four more times. Then she opened her eyes and was chagrined to discover her migraine had advanced to the next stage. In the center of her gaze floated the dark spot of nothingness that usually preceded the nausea. She held her hand up in front of her face but saw only her fingertips. The palm appeared to be curiously nonexistent.

"Robot pa-rade," Casey sang tunelessly from the back seat. Michelle glanced into the rear view but found that she could not see him. There was only a dark circular void where her son should have been.

Michelle pressed the release button on her safety belt and opened her door and opened her door with a sigh. Then she opened the back door and leaned in to unbuckle Casey.

"I don't wanna go in!" the boy complained.

Michelle paused, considering. *I could be in and out in less than five minutes.* Then she shook her head slightly and withdrew her protesting son from his car seat. Casey kicked and tried to wriggle away.

"I wanna stay here!"

"You have to come in with Mommy. I can't leave you in the car or some strange man might try to steal you."

Casey abruptly stopped fussing. "What strange man?"

"I don't know." Michelle walked with him toward the drug store's entrance. "Maybe there's someone hiding somewhere."

The automatic doors slid open and Michelle and Casey stepped into the drug store's fluorescent interior. The dowdy cashier looked up briefly, nodded a hello and continued scanning items for a bored looking bearded man in a Buffalo Bills T-shirt.

Michelle glanced at the local newspaper rack. The headline read: "State Homeless Numbers Up". Other headlines above the fold included a fatal car crash out on the Interstate and the search for a lost hiker in the nearby national forest. Michelle shook her head. Seemed like nothing but bad news. She felt afraid to find out what tomorrow's headline might be.

Her vision had cleared but now the pain was starting to creep into the base of her skull. Tendrils of burning discomfort would soon shoot through her brain. Every second counted. The pharmacy was tucked into the corner on the opposite end of the store and Michelle took Casey's hand and headed in that direction.

The pair had to stop at the intersection of aisles for the tallest woman Michelle had seen in years. The woman looked as if she stood about six foot four. She had wiry gray hair and a stern expression. Her cart was filled to capacity with cartons of diet soda. The woman plodded past and Michelle caught sight of her companion; another elderly woman barely over five feet tall, her hair dyed a garish orange hue. A small package of facial tissue made up the entire contents of the cart she was pushing. Stifling a giggle, despite the increasing discomfort of her migraine, Michelle continued down the aisle.

"Mom, can I go look at the toys?" Casey wrested his hand from hers.

"Will you be good and stay right here until I come back?"

"Yes."

"And you promise not to talk to strangers?"

"Yes."

Michelle sighed. Nausea was setting in. "I'll be in the next row."

"Okay," Casey replied absently, already gazing at the colorful diecast cars in their little blue packages.

Michelle rounded the corner and accidentally brushed against a man standing in the next aisle. He was of average build, short cropped brown hair and unremarkable features. The only memorable trait the man could boast were his light green eyes, which held Michelle's gaze for a moment before a wave of dizziness swept over her. Michelle staggered and everything briefly went black. She fumbled out a hand to steady herself, sending several plastic bottles of vitamins clattering to the tile floor.

Michelle kept her eyes closed and waited for the dizzy spell to pass. She opened her eyes to see the pharmacist staring at her from behind his counter. The man she had bumped into was nowhere in sight.

She gave the pharmacist what she hoped was a reassuring smile. "I'm all right," Michelle croaked in a hoarse voice that she hardly recognized. Embarrassed, she stooped to pick up the bottles.

"It's okay, I'll get them." The pharmacist came around the counter.

Michelle nodded and moved self-consciously down the aisle to the headache medicine. There was one brand that worked rather well on her migraines and Michelle scanned the shelf for it. She stopped short, amazed.

Michelle no longer felt the tendrils of pain encroaching on her temples or the base of her neck. Her vision was fine and she didn't feel any nausea either. Her migraine had miraculously disappeared. Michelle realized that after bumping into the man with the striking green eyes, her migraine symptoms left her. Smiling to herself, she strode back to the toy aisle.

"Casey..." she rasped. Michelle started to clear the frog from her throat then froze. Casey wasn't there. A tidal wave of panic rose and washed away her irritation at seeing that he'd wandered away. She immediately turned and looked in all four directions. A little red-haired girl followed her mother down one aisle. The other aisles antagonized her by being empty.

As she turned the corner at the end of the aisle, Michelle reflected that bad things happened to people—even children—all the time. She silently prayed that nothing bad had happened to Casey. Michelle moved toward the cash registers, looking carefully down each aisle as she passed. She saw the tall and short elderly women still caravanning together in one aisle and a stock boy opening boxes halfway down another. A man and a woman, obviously a couple, browsed the magazine rack. No Casey.

Then Michelle realized something that made her feel like she had been kicked in the stomach: she hadn't seen the green-eyed man she had bumped into. Had he heard her telling Casey to wait? She had practically announced to anyone listening that the boy would be unattended. Michelle mentally cursed herself and broke into a panicky jog, heading to where the register lanes and the entrance were located.

There! Michelle saw the back of Casey's head. He was walking toward the exit.

"Casey!" Michelle shouted. Her voice again sounded strange in her own ears. Her son turned and stared in her direction. His mouth hung open and his eyes were wide.

"Casey, you stay right there!" Michelle rasped. "I'm coming to get you."

A look of terror altered her son's features and he turned and ran. He was gone out the front door before she could circumvent the customers crowded with their carts at the checkout lines.

Frustration overwhelmed Michelle and she screamed, "Stop running!"

She jostled through the crowd, furious that no one seemed to care about her situation. In fact, several customers peered suspiciously at her and two even gave her dirty looks as she pushed past them.

Michelle could see out the sliding glass doors and into the parking lot now. Casey was being carried toward a dark windowless van by a woman wearing the same outfit Michelle had worn today.

"STOP!" she shrieked in terror as she neared the automatic doors. The glass slid open but before Michelle could pass through, something large and hard drove into her hip and sent her sprawling. Michelle crashed into the local newspaper rack and then fell to the tile floor. Pain shot through her right elbow and her left hip throbbed.

Stunned, she looked up to see the tall gray-haired woman towering above, glowering at her.

The diminutive orange haired woman pursed her lips disapprovingly. "You got him, Agatha."

"Probably some pree-vert," the tall woman said, her eyes never leaving Michelle.

A man with a bad comb-over and a green vest hurried up. "I've phoned the police."

"Get out there and stop that van!" Michelle motioned frantically with one hand as she struggled to her feet. A group of grim-faced customers barred her path to the exit.

"I don't think so, buddy," the man who had been in the magazine aisle with his wife replied.

"Get out of the way!" Michelle growled. She wondered again at the strangeness of her voice.

The manager stepped closer. "Just stay calm and we'll get this all sorted out. We don't need any trouble."

"That woman has my son!" Michelle appealed.

The cashier who had nodded hello shook her head. "No sir, that little boy came in with his mama and he left with his mama."

Michelle began to tremble. This was insane. It couldn't be happening. Then Michelle thought about her voice again. A vague idea formed.

"May I walk down your cosmetics aisle while we wait for the police to arrive?" Michelle tried very hard to appear calm, but the sound of her voice made her want to scream.

The store manager looked at Michelle closely and finally nodded. The crowd parted and Michelle strode carefully through the aisle until she found the rack of lipstick testers. Above the testers was a small mirror for customers use when trying out colors.

Michelle took a deep breath and looked in the mirror. A stranger stared back at her. Short cropped brown hair framed an unremarkable male face. Bright green eyes returned Michelle's gaze. She staggered back and began to scream. She screamed until her vocal cords simply refused to produce any more sound.

It took six people just to hold her down until a police officer arrived.

#

Michelle awoke in a hospital bed. A policeman sat in a chair in the corner of the tiny room. Michelle guessed that he was there to guard her but was staring raptly at the television on the opposite wall instead. She glanced at the screen and saw that the local news was on.

"Looks like we owe you an apology, sir." The policeman sounded awestruck. "How in the hell did you know she was gonna kill her kid?"

Michelle looked up and saw herself on the television screen. She wore an orange jumpsuit and manacles on her hands and feet. She struggled as police wrestled her into the back of a police cruiser. Michelle's heart seemed to jump in her chest as the woman on the screen turned and shouted directly at the camera. "I'm the arresting officer!" she cried. "She switched bodies with me!" The door of the police cruiser slammed and the woman's cries became inaudible.

"That woman is crazier than an outhouse rat!" the policeman remarked.

The news anchor was speaking again. "A closed-casket memorial service will be held for Casey Watkins this Friday at…"

Michelle stopped listening. When her husband died in combat in Iraq, Casey had become her everything, her reason for living. And now that reason was gone. Her every fiber of being felt scorched and desolate. For Michelle, only the formality of the actual act of dying remained.

She beckoned to the policeman, who stood up and moved toward her, his eyebrows raised in a quizzical expression. Michelle's eyes darted to the enticing black steel handle of the Beretta holstered on his hip and watched as it got closer... closer...

BEDTIME STORIES FOR CARRION BEETLES

SOLITARY MAN

Hello Tyler. It's Dad. I'm sorry your mother isn't with me. Seeing you in here like this is awful hard on her. You know how she got last time. Most mothers faced with this situation, you expect them to break down. Crying and carrying on. But screaming and blaming the paramedics, the other driver, and even God until she foamed at the mouth? I didn't think she had it in her.

I thought it'd be best to leave her at home. You understand. Besides, it'll give me a chance to visit with you about my work. You've shown an interest before but I've always kept what goes on in prison to myself. I never took the time to tell you about my job and now I wish I had. Despite your state, I can't help but think that it's not too late. That maybe something I tell you today will get through to you somehow.

I'll tell you about the prisoners on death row another time. Ditto for the yard fights and some of the contraband we've found smuggled in. Believe me, I have a lot of stories I could tell. But tonight I want to tell you about the block. A few of the guys call it 'the cooler' and the official term for an area that I'm in charge of is 'solitary confinement'. It's a special form of imprisonment where the prisoner is denied contact with any of the other prisoner and doesn't get any visitation. Most prisons do allow for minimal contact with staff; guards conduct room searches and somebody cleans every once in a while. But I run a tighter operation. The only contact the prisoners in the block have is with me. And I can be pretty tight-lipped when I want to be.

The prisoner holding the record for longest stay on the block under my watch is this guy who beheaded a Catholic priest in the late 1970s. He never gives me any trouble—he's a model prisoner actually—but any time we tried to move him back into the general population, guys would try to kill him. Usually the Irish Catholics, but the Hispanics can be really religious too. So this guy stays in the kind of protective custody that only the block can supply.

There are other prisoners confined to the block. Crazy bastards who relish the chance to inflict suffering. Loose cannons with faulty wiring. But they're not the ones I want to tell you about either.

I keep dancing around the subject and I don't know why.

There's one prisoner in particular that I want to tell someone about. I need to get it off my chest. Part of it is your old man wanting to clear his conscience. But another part of it is me needing to understand just what the hell is going on.

This prisoner, he's quite famous. He's a writer. Specializes in horror and mysteries. He's cracked the bestseller list several times. Let me whisper his name...

Maybe you recognize him, maybe you don't. I guess I have to admit I don't know if you're much of a reader or not. But this author, he's always shunned the spotlight. He refuses interviews and he's never done a single book signing. Hell, his publisher doesn't even print his photo on the dust jackets because they don't have one!

But he's got a cult following like you wouldn't believe. Awards, accolades, respectable sales...he still gets it all. You know why? Because nobody knows he's in prison! His fans think he's a recluse, like that guy who wrote 'Catcher in the Rye'. Only a handful of people— his agent, his editor at the publisher, the previous warden here and me—knew that one of America's most popular horror and mystery authors got himself incarcerated with no hope of parole. Think on that for a bit.

None of his fans know it, but this guy was convicted of premeditated first degree murder ten years ago. He was sentenced to life without parole but no one ever knew. Know why? Because money talks. His publisher spent a fortune keeping the whole thing a secret. I'm not saying the system is corrupt; if it was, he would have walked away a free man. I'm saying sometimes certain exceptions are made.

You know what he told me when he first arrived? Said he just needed to know that what he was writing was realistic. Can you imagine? Said he did it "for love of the craft". Not the craft of murder, but writing. Told me now that he'd experienced it for himself, he could write for the rest of his career and never worry about the quality of his output. I just shook my head and told him he'd never get to write again.

Was I ever wrong!

His editor at the publisher made a deal with the old warden. It was all under the table and the powers-that-be were incredibly guarded when it came to who knew what. The public was—and still is—hungry for new books by this guy and I have a key part in making it happen. My cut over the last ten years has paid your college tuition—if you ever go.

I know by now you must be wondering what it is that I do for this author exactly. My only duty is to smuggle in paper each day and pens whenever he needs them.

A lot of the guards are on the take, either turning a blind eye to certain situations or bringing in contraband on their own to make some extra cash. I never got involved with any of that. But this was, and still is, a whole different set of circumstances. So one day this guy in a suit shows up in the parking lot and offers to buy me coffee. Turns out he's the author's agent. Flew all the way here just to visit me personally. He laid it all out that day: I get a package once a month; a ream of paper, a few pens, and stamped, addressed manila envelopes.

Whenever the prisoner completes a new story or a chapter in his latest novel, I slip it into one of the envelopes and drop it in the mail. His latest book got him a Stoker nomination. I read the first draft before anyone, including his agent and his editor.

Not that I'm gloating. I'm taking a serious risk doing what I'm doing. It's gotten more dangerous now that there are fewer of us who know about the arrangement. The warden the publisher made the deal with passed away last winter and the new warden's not in the loop. I'm the only guy they really need inside when you think about it. I'm the only person he has any contact with in the block. The author's agent knows but the original editor died a few years ago and as far as his new editor and the staff at the publisher knows the author's just a recluse. So I'm mostly responsible for keeping this guy's work on the best seller lists.

It feels good to tell you all of this. There are worse things I could do, don't get me wrong. But to finally confide in someone, well, it feels good like I said. I guess I'm a little selfish in telling you but part of me thought you might be interested in my famous—but secret—prisoner.

I also thought you might relate to him a little bit. I mean, he's in there, locked up in solitary confinement. We don't ever directly communicate. He is truly alone. Like you, Son. Locked away some place where it seems that no one can reach you.

BEDTIME STORIES FOR CARRION BEETLES

How you even lived through the accident is nothing short of a miracle. It's not too often a motorcycle rider survives a collision with an eighteen wheeler. The doctors say you might wake up tomorrow...or not at all. So I wanted to tell you the story about the man cut off from everyone and yet he still manages to thrill readers with his words all these years later. That's really an amazing accomplishment. If you can hear me Tyler, I hope it helps you cope, even just a little. If you can hear me, know that your mother and I—and a lot of other folks out here—hope you can find your way back to us. We hope to be hearing from you again real soon.

Speaking of your mother, she's probably got supper on the table and is wondering where I am and what's keeping me. I just wanted to stop by after work to talk for a spell. One more thing, Tyler; this is the part that really has your old man completely confounded.

This famous author...he's been on the block under my care for ten years now. But I haven't actually entered his cell in quite some time. I don't even look in there any more. I'm too *afraid* to. Every day I bring him his meals and his smuggled paper on a flat tray that I slide through this narrow horizontal slot in his cell door. And every day like clockwork I'm there to get the pages and the meal tray when the prisoner pushes them back out.

The pages are always full, front and back, with handwritten lines every time. But for the past four and a half years, the food on the trays gets returned untouched.

WIND, WINTER, WENDIGO

I.

To call the winter of 1889 a harsh one for the residents of the tiny community of Wind, Minnesota, would be an understatement.

Milo Odens died first. Dr. Larken had diagnosed Milo with consumption and indicated that due to its advanced stage, there was nothing to be done. He'd tried to prescribe laudanum, but Milo refused to stoop to such an indignity. He bore his suffering and faced his impending death with the stoicism of his pioneer lineage.

Milo's wife, Margaret, and son, Jacob, returned in the wagon from Sunday service to find Milo crumpled on the farmhouse steps. They were sure he was dead, but he wasn't. Not yet. The man struggled into a sitting position as his family hurried toward him.

"Margaret," His throat made a wet gurgle. "Run inside and fetch a sheet.

"Milo—" Margaret began.

He feebly raised a hand, silencing her.

"I'm going fast, woman, and you'll want the sheet to cover me," he said. Then he added more quietly, "It's the decent Christian thing to do."

Margaret turned as white as the sheet she would eventually bring. Her face crumpled at the significance of his words, but her husband's matter-of-fact tone set her feet in motion across the frozen ground.

Milo watched her go. Then he turned to his son. Summoning all his remaining strength, he grabbed the front of the boy's frock and pulled him close until they were eye to eye.

"Heed my words, boy! Make sure you see him lay me in the ground!" Milo spoke these last words vehemently, giving the boy a shake at the end for added emphasis.

Jacob nodded. To him, this seemed a strange and unnecessary request. Milo released his grip as a coughing fit wracked his body.

Despite the chill, Jacob removed his coat and rolled it into a makeshift pillow for his father's head, but Milo pushed it away. He attempted to speak but another coughing spell seized him.

A fine spray of dark blood spattered the boy's exposed shirt sleeves. Jacob stared at his arms despondently as the droplets soaked into the white fabric.

"I think my Sunday shirt is ruined, Pa," he said, still gazing down at his sleeves.

He looked up again into the glassy eyes of a dead man. At the age of ten, Jacob Odens realized he'd become the man of the house.

II.

A winter blizzard struck like an angry rattlesnake the next day. The residents of Wind hunkered down and coped as best they could. Bitter winds tore through the barren fields and the snow seemed to have nowhere to land. Anyone with a lively imagination might have said the snow flakes twisted and capered through the sky like icy Nordic demons, but no one in the town of Wind had much of an imagination.

The frozen ground refused to accept the blade of the undertaker's shovel. Although no one came right out and told Margaret, her late husband's body would have to spend the winter stored in the shed belonging to the undertaker, Wendell Ghoh. A memorial service had already been held and it was understood that the undertaker would perform a hasty burial when spring thaws allowed.

Phil Tolsma, owner of the general store, did brisk business selling blankets and such. No matter how bad the weather, the mercantile always contained patrons. Tolsma's store was often inhabited by a handful of the town's most notable men. This group consisted of the town's oldest resident, Rudolph van de Waal; the richest man, Carl Wayne; the newspaper editor Ernest de Roos; and the town sheriff, Garret Barrows. Phil Tolsma would often join them as they sat around the wood stove in Tolsma's General Store, swapping stories and looking wise. It was Ernest de Roos who first heard about Caleb Grant.

He'd died not more than twenty yards from his front door, according to de Roos, who made the announcement with a trace of morbid delight. This was juicy news. Caleb Grant's mind wasn't as sharp as it had been in his younger days. He'd obviously misjudged the wind chill factor by at least twenty degrees. Caleb's closest neighbor found his body hunched over a fallen tree, ax still clutched in his frozen hand. Caleb Grant joined Milo Odens in Wendell Ghoh's shed.

As the days wore on, the wind continued its assault on the land. Snow didn't fall; it was whipped to the ground by the wind. Even the barrel-chested Melvin Gerlach described walking in the storm akin to being peppered with buckshot.

Spring seemed an eternity away.

III.

Two weeks later, Melvin and Myrna Gerlach's little girl, Holly, died of pneumonia. Jacob and his mother were in town the day the weeping couple happened to drive by in their wagon. Jacob had been tending to the horses while his mother shopped inside the mercantile when they passed. Drawn by a combination of reverence and boyish curiosity, Jacob followed at a discreet distance to the undertaker's. The boy watched in horrified fascination as the stricken father carried his daughter for the last time. Ghoh was there, of course, holding the shed door open and looking on as if he couldn't wait for the grieving parents to be gone. While many of the residents of Wind forgave his detached and emotionless manner as a necessity of his calling, Jacob found himself appalled by the undertaker's demeanor.

Jacob removed his hat respectfully as the Gerlachs drove past him again, returning to a home that would seem hollow to the grieving parents. When they were out of sight, the boy crept toward the undertaker's shed. He knew this was where Ghoh kept the cadavers safely frozen until winter relinquished its grip on the land.

As Jacob drew nearer, a bitter wind rattled the shed door. Had Ghoh left it unfastened? Inside the shed, someone groaned. Curious, Jacob eased up to the door and peered in through the crack. His eyes had trouble adjusting to the shed's dim interior but his ears confirmed the presence of someone moaning. Jacob started to dimly make out the tall form of the undertaker bending over something in the far corner. Jacob watched the undertaker's hands lift from what he now recognized as Holly Gerlach's body. Was Ghoh weeping and covering his face with his hands? Perhaps Jacob had misjudged the man, who was now practically prostrate over the dead girl.

Feeling ashamed for intruding, Jacob cast about the shed until his gaze fell on a larger form under a burlap feed sack closer to the entrance. For the first time the boy realized he might see his father's earthly remains and he faltered, but that couldn't possibly be his father. For one thing, the form resembled a grown man only until the waist; then the burlap sagged down to the wood plank. That person, whoever it had been, didn't have any legs.

A gaunt white face, livid with anger, abruptly filled his field of vision and Jacob cried out. Ghoh loomed over him, seeming to cast writhing shadows in every direction and Jacob tumbled backwards into the snow. Wendell Ghoh's mouth looked like a wet, red gash as he screamed, "Get out of here!"

Jacob scrambled to his feet and fled, leaving white puffs of breath floating in the air like a departing locomotive.

IV.

"Best be getting to those horses, Jacob," Margaret Odens said as she wearily cleared the supper dishes from the table.

"Yes, Ma," the boy replied. He needed no reminding that Ugoljok and Veterok needed grain and water. He'd probably need to fork some extra straw for the horses to bed down in as well. It would be another dangerously cold night.

Jacob hitched up his coveralls and shrugged into a heavy wool coat. Thick gloves covered his hands and he pulled a knitted cap down over his forehead.

The howling arctic wind hit Jacob full in the face as he pulled the door closed behind him. Head bent, he trudged toward the barn which stabled the family's horses.

Jacob's father had been very proud of them; he even insisted on keeping the names the previous owner (a blustering Russian named Danil) had given them. "Ugoljok and Veterok are names with strength and majesty, Jacob." Milo had said. "Translating them to Blackie and Breezy makes 'em sound like kittens."

Caring for the horses was not only a necessity; it also provided Jacob with a means of honoring his father's memory.

As Jacob approached the barn, he became aware of an intermittent pounding coming from inside. He lifted the latch and quickly slid open the doors. Veterok bucked in her stall, kicking the boards with her rear hooves. The boy's eyes scanned Ugoljok's stall but did not find him there.

Then Jacob spied part of the black stallion's flank. Ugoljok was sprawled on the ground behind the stacked bales of straw. Running forward, the boy uttered a choked cry. Ugoljok was obviously dead, his neck torn out. It looked like a bloody length of fire hose draining the last of its contents in feeble spurts. As Jacob stood staring at the gaping wound, his skin began to prickle. Veterok emitted a loud whinny and reared up again, eyes bulging in terror. A claw-like hand grabbed Jacob's shoulder like a vise. The boy drew in his breath to shout, but was thrust sideways, roughly hitting the boards of Ugoljok's vacant stall before he could cry out.

His head exploded with stars and he collapsed to the ground. Jacob's vision blurred as the dark figure loomed over him.

"So hungry..." the towering specter moaned, sounding both sorrowful and greedy. The rank stench of death seemed to emanate from the trespasser. Jacob's blood ran cold with revulsion and he began to scream.

Veterok shattered two of the boards holding her in. They flew out at the tall figure standing over Jacob. The blow would have knocked any other man sprawling, but Jacob's would-be attacker only staggered briefly. Veterok galloped past and reared in the corner of the barn, whinnying fearfully. The creature turned and seemed to consider chasing the horse when a harsh voice cut the night.

"Step away from my boy or you're dead where you stand, Mister."

Jacob recognized his mother's voice and shook his head, trying to clear it. For one split second, the towering form in the barn stood motionless. Then it exploded forward. Margaret was not used to handling a shotgun and the intruder roughly knocked her aside with an arcing swipe of his left arm. The errant shotgun blast was deafening in the confines of the barn and debris raining down from the roof showed where the buckshot had struck. Jacob raced to the barn door but his mother caught him and held him in a clinging embrace. He could only watch the fleeing shape disappear with astonishing speed into the dark woods.

V.

Sheriff Barrows and a few other men from town came out the next day to drag Ugoljok's remains out behind the barn about fifty yards. Then they covered it with brush. Jacob was beside himself with frustration. He felt like he'd let his father down. As he crunched across the frozen ground toward the chopping block that evening, the boy tried to rationalize his guilt.

How could he have known someone would sneak into their barn and kill one of their horses?

Jacob began to chop firewood, his breath emitting a white puff with each swing of the ax.

He wanted to do something as a tribute. On the surface it would be a gesture for the horse, but the boy was introspective enough to know he really wanted to somehow memorialize his father.

Jacob stood another log up and swung the ax. The log cracked, fell in two and Jacob reached for another.

He couldn't bury Ugoljok; the ground was frozen solid. The boy reflected on this, hefting the ax. *Pa's not even buried yet. He's still in—*

The boy's mouth fell open in disbelief. The ax slid from his hand and thumped on the ground. Jacob realized he knew who had been lurking in the barn the night before and who had killed Ugoljok. He'd been face to face with that blood-smeared visage before and not even realized what he had seen.

To Jacob, the truth seemed like a hornet's nest. Every realization that sprang from the truth was another angry hornet planting a stinger in him. Some penetrated his brain, others pierced his heart.

VI.

Two days later, Margaret and Jacob Odens made the frigid journey to town again. The trip took longer than usual now that they had only one horse to pull the wagon. Jacob's own state of nervous excitement made the trek seem to last even longer.

Once they'd arrived in Wind, Jacob nearly danced in place, listening to his mother's instructions. He was to take the list she had made to Tolsma's General Store while she attended to some business at the bank. Jacob nodded and nearly ran to the entrance of the mercantile.

Inside, the store was empty save for the usual group, huddled in their accustomed places around the wood stove. Old Rudolph van de Waal was there, his gnarled hands idly stroking the cane he used. Carl Wayne was there and Sheriff Barrows leaned back in his customary chair, arms folded. Ernest de Roos paused from filling his pipe long enough to nod at the boy, then returned to his activity without another glance. Phil Tolsma asked if the boy needed any help. Jacob politely declined, saying his mother would be there shortly. The shopkeeper shrugged and sat down with the others.

Jacob found one or two items on the list and then could stand it no longer. This might be his only opportunity to speak freely about his suspicions before his mother entered.

He approached the group, feeling shy now. He cleared his throat. "Wendell Ghoh killed my horse."

Sheriff Barrows grunted. Most of the others seemed to ignore him completely. Only de Roos, the newspaperman, looked up. He smiled at Jacob indulgently.

"How's that now?" he asked.

"Wendell Ghoh, the undertaker," Jacob said. He suddenly felt short of breath. "I saw him in my barn that night. He knocked me down and ran off. He is the one who killed Ugoljok."

The men all stared at him now. Their expressions ranged from frank disbelief to sardonic humor. Jacob felt his face flush under their scrutiny.

"He said he was hungry," he finished lamely.

The men surrounding the stove chuckled. Rudy van de Waal slapped his knee and pounded his cane on the floor for effect. Jacob grimly pressed on.

"I think he's crazy. I don't think my father or any of the other people who have passed away should be in Wendell Ghoh's shed until spring."

"So the town undertaker is a horse killer? Is that your assertion?" Ernest de Roos sounded like a courtroom lawyer cross-examining a witness, and the room erupted again.

"He's an evil man and I'll prove it somehow," Jacob gritted his teeth angrily. "I'll just have to show you if you don't believe me!"

At the sound of boards creaking outside the door, Jacob whirled and resumed filling his arms with items from the list. Margaret Odens noticed nothing amiss as she entered the store and joined her son in their shopping.

VII.

Four days later, a small bundled-up figure crept from the Odens' house and into the moonlit night. The figure entered the barn and rode away on Veterok.

Near dawn, Veterok returned to the farm, head down and walking slow. The horse was exhausted, famished and nearly frozen.

She had no rider.

VIII.

The first spring thaw brought with it a flurry of activity at the cemetery. Wendell Ghoh amazed everyone in town with his energetic digging. Somehow overnight, graves were dug for all those citizens who had passed away during the winter. Although the body of Jacob Odens was never found, several other Wind residents were interred in Wendell Ghoh's shed. Spinster Mary Ellen Mason took ill and passed away just after the first of the year. And Rudy van de Waal himself breathed his last in early February.

Wendell Ghoh did all the digging himself. No one in town helped him dig and no one had been called upon to help carry the caskets to burial.

On the day Margaret Odens walked in to Tolsma's General Store for the last time, the same group of familiar faces circled around the stove. It wasn't lit, but habits are hard to break.

"Sorry to see you go," Carl Wayne offered.

"Can't say as I blame ya." This came from Melvin Gerlach, who knew something of loss himself.

"Say hello to the folks back east," Ernest de Roos said.

"Thank you all," Margaret replied. There was no color in her cheeks, no glimmer in her eyes. "I won't be coming back."

Melvin Gerlach nodded. Phil Tolsma grunted and idly scratched his cheek.

"I won't need a horse in Chicago, so I gave Veterok away." Margaret looked at each of the men in turn. "Since he's been so helpful first with Milo, and then with the memorial he constructed for... for Jacob..."

Margaret broke off, sobbed once and regained control. She swallowed hard and continued. "To repay his kindness, I gave Veterok to Mr. Ghoh."

Sheriff Barrows' eyes bulged briefly, like he'd swallowed a walnut, shell and all. He tried to speak, found that he couldn't, and looked out the window instead.

The silence spun out awkwardly.

At the distant sound of the approaching train whistle, Margaret stooped to pick up her luggage. Melvin Gerlach jumped to his feet to help. He picked up the heaviest of the suitcases and waited outside, holding the door for her.

The other men didn't seem to know where to look. Mystified at their odd behavior, Margaret cast one more backward glance at the abashed men then walked through the front door of the mercantile and out of their lives forever.

The collective stubbornness of the men hung in the air like suffocating gauze, yet no one broke the silence.

Though the group as a whole shared a common secret, bonding them inexorably together, each suffered from his own accusatory thoughts alone.

IX.

Wind was not an easy place to live and it was widely recognized as a place where a lot more folks died than were born. The hard winters accounted for many of the deaths, but those who lived in Wind and the surrounding area seemed prone to all manner of fatal accidents. More than one person abandoned their family and left town unannounced, never to be heard from again. That was the general belief, at any rate.

Through it all, gaunt old Wendell Ghoh served the community faithfully. The toll of his endless work always showed in his haunted, haggard eyes. They darted back and forth, keenly examining everyone he encountered. The citizens of Wind noticed that he always inquired about the health of one person or the habits of another. It was as if he were always searching for the town cemetery's next arrival.

"Nancy Downie fell out of her wagon and broke her neck yesterday and Wendell was there before her body had time to cool," Phil Tolsma announced one afternoon.

"Takes his job very seriously," Carl Wayne commented. The others nodded.

"We're lucky to have him," Melvin Gerlach said amid murmurs of assent.

"He missed his true calling as a doctor," Sheriff Garret Barrows declared.

The residents of the town continued to lie to each other and to themselves. The years passed and the population dwindled.

Such is the curse of the Wendigo.

COLD FEET

Even though I work with cadavers every day, *I'm* the one with cold feet!

I'll explain that in a moment, Doctor Mayes, but first I want to express how surprised I am at meeting you here. I realize I don't have an appointment and the circumstances are unusual, but being able to talk to you once more would really mean so much to me right now. You've helped me through tough times before and I sure could use your advice.

You see, about six months ago I asked Holly to marry me. She agreed and I was ecstatic...for a while. The problem is, now that the wedding is only a few weeks away, I'm having serious second thoughts.

Not Holly, though. She's been running around as busy as a bee, making the final arrangements—

Oh my God. I can't believe I just said that. *Final arrangements.* You'd think I was talking about a funeral. Let's see if I can choose my words more carefully this time: Holly has been seeing to the last-minute details of our nuptials.

As for me, I've been spending more and more time alone, mulling things over.

I know what you're thinking. *'What could possibly rattle Bill March, the senior mortician at Carlton Funeral Chapel?'* Maybe I'm jumping to conclusions and subconsciously creating excuses so that I don't have to go through with the marriage. I'll let you be the judge...

A year and a half ago, when she first started her apprenticeship at Carlton, Holly and I hit it off immediately. Her first day on the job, she brought some compact discs in from her car. We embalmed our first cadaver together with a movie soundtrack composed by Angelo Badalamenti playing in the background.

As I've already told you, I felt an attraction to Holly from day one. I love her eyes. Picture a young Leeza Gibbons and you have a good idea of what my fiancé looks like. Holly's hair is blond. I'd like it better if she'd grow it out and just tie it back when she's working but she keeps it cut short instead. Maybe that's something I can get her to change once we're married.

Holly has an adorable button nose and very kissable lips. A little like she's pouting, but not a collagen disaster. She gets her eyebrows waxed in a way that really accentuates her eyes. I think her eyes, eyelids and eyebrows are her best features. Did I mention that already? Sorry, I guess I'm a little fixated. As you have pointed out on more than one occasion, Doctor, I have a tendency to obsess.

See there? A little self-recognition. I *have* been paying attention during our sessions!

But let me get back to my fiancé.

I don't mean to brag, but Holly has a great body too. I'd say she's smoking hot.

I remember one evening, as we were cleaning up a high school kid who'd been ejected from his pickup during a rollover; Holly asked me what one characteristic about her I would change if I could. I guess lots of guys would have made the smart response and said *'nothing'* but I told her that she could stand to lose some weight. She didn't get mad or fall to pieces over it, just quietly went about her work. Afterward, I felt bad about it, but she didn't bring it up again so neither did I.

For a long time, my sense of professionalism kept me from making any moves on her. I've never been a guy who condones romantic entanglements at work. Not with the staff, not with the families and definitely not with the clients. (That last part was a joke, of course.)

We had gone to dinner a few times but I could never quite bring myself to proposition her, much less propose. A little voice in the back of my head kept finding things wrong with her looks or her personality. Don't get me wrong, I *wanted* to be attracted to her, but stuff like her weight had a negative effect.

I realize I must sound like a shallow jerk, but look at it this way: If you were five-foot-two and your prom date was six feet tall, would it make you feel uncomfortable? Of course it would. Now imagine spending the rest of your life in a situation like that. That's how it was with Holly and me. Now, I know what you're thinking: I'm fixating on one characteristic and obsessing over it. I'm really trying to work on that, I swear. That's why I'm talking to you now.

Professionally speaking, Holly has progressed in her skill level as an apprentice to the point where she has less than six months to go before she earns her license. Then I'd like to make her a full partner. Here at the funeral home I mean, but I suppose you could say that phrase applies in our personal lives too. Sometimes our professional and personal lives overlap. There was one time—and I do want to stress that it was *one time*—where things spiraled out of control and our physical desires invaded the sanctity of this room.

It was a warm spring evening, just a few months after we had started dating. We'd completed embalming a stroke victim and had transported the casket upstairs to the chapel for a late evening viewing. Since another funeral director would be overseeing the viewing, Holly and I returned to wash up before heading home. I guess we both had spring fever, because I found myself kissing her at the cleanup sink. She kissed me back and we both got pretty worked up. Then she said, "Come over here; I want to show you something." I followed her over to one of the mortuary cots and she positioned herself on it so that her head was hanging down off the back of it. Then she directed me to unzip and she...

Sorry, Doctor. There's a lot more I could tell but I don't think it would be appropriate. Suffice it to say that my bride-to-be is not hindered by any gag reflex, if you catch my drift. That's a rare and cherished quality, in my opinion.

But enough of that subject.

Let's talk about you for a moment, shall we? Your family has my deepest sympathies, of course. And now you are here as my client, instead of vice versa. I hope you will forgive my sneaking in one more session with you before we part ways, but I must have your professional opinion.

I hope you will forgive me commenting on your state but I am surprised at how good you still look. When one hears about an accident involving a convertible and an eighteen-wheeler, one doesn't expect to have much left to work with! You will be pleased to know that if I can overcome one key hurdle, I should be able to present you in an open casket for your memorial.

You'd be appalled at the state of some of the cadavers that we see rolling in here. Embalming is really a balance of art and science and you have to possess a naturally strong stomach for this kind of work, believe me. After a few bad car accidents or burn victims, you develop a stomach of steel. Holly was a natural from day one. She never had to leave the room, no matter what condition the cadaver was in.

The same can be said for me, although to a lesser extent. It depends on the situation. For instance, Holly's strong stomach extends to meal time too. Me? I'm a burger and fries kind of guy. Or steak and potatoes, if we're dining fancy. But Holly goes for all kinds of food I'd never touch. You know that sushi bar that opened a few months ago on Mason Lane? My fiancé loves it. Who in their right mind eats raw fish wrapped in seaweed? It's disgusting. She watches that show on cable with the guy who travels all over the world eating bizarre food. I get so grossed out I have to leave the room.

Talking about that reminds me of the time we almost ran for the door here at work. It was the only time I can remember where we both got rattled while processing a cadaver. Now that I think about it, that day marked a turning point in our relationship. Mostly for the good, but sometimes I wonder.

The deceased had expired of natural causes. Her name was Minnie Markowitz and she was one hundred and four years old when she died. Not trying to make you feel jealous. I'm sure you've lived a full life, too. But the reason I bring up her age is because Holly and I got to talking about it as we worked. Minnie's sixty-year-old grandson was writing the check for everything. He nearly talked my ear off as we filled out paperwork and made the final arrangements. According to him, Minnie had been something of a sex symbol in her day. She'd started as a burlesque dancer, moved to acting in films when 'talkies' were new, and had gone on to star in several Broadway shows. He told me her stage name and if I told you, you'd probably recognize her. Unfortunately the details slip my mind.

Even after Minnie finally 'retired' she didn't stay out of the limelight. Her slender figure was legendary, and as long as she kept it, Minnie still made plenty of television and public appearances. But she was more than just a celebrity.

She got involved in charity work, took an interest in politics and championed a number of humanitarian causes.

I got all this from her grandson as he sat reminiscing in my office. It's something I always let the clients do. It helps with the grieving process. Anyway, he talked about how her mind was still sharp, but that she had slowed down noticeably near the end. He said she felt weaker and more exhausted with each passing day. He told me that Minnie admitted that she *'couldn't stay ahead of it any more.'* At the time, I thought that was her way of saying she couldn't keep up with the pace of life. I found out I was wrong.

The outside temperature was scorching and we had the air conditioning cranked as we unzipped a black bag containing the late Minnie Markowitz. Wrinkles had made a road map of her face, but otherwise she was still a beautiful and regal looking woman, even at one hundred and four. Her clothing and personal effects had already been removed and inventoried.

Holly kept smiling to herself as she briefly lifted each eyelid to check Minnie's corneas for clouding. I placed a modesty cloth across our subject's lap and asked Holly what was so funny.

"Nothing's funny," she said. "I'm just impressed that she lived to such a ripe old age—and she doesn't look half bad."

"Chalk that up to the 'Everything in Moderation, Including Moderation' philosophy," I replied. "According to her grandson, Minnie drank, smoked and ate like a horse right up to the end."

"Good for you, honey," Holly addressed the cadaver as she began washing the body with disinfectant solution.

The arterial embalming went smoothly and after that we started the cavity embalming procedure. (You'll experience all that for yourself shortly.) Holly stepped away briefly and changed the disc. She grinned impishly as the soft piano of Ravel's *Pavane Pour Une Infante Defunte* filled the room and I rolled my eyes at the irony of her selection.

"Hey, this one's for Minnie." Holly put her hands on her hips. "Young at heart 'til the end."

I grinned and selected a scalpel from the tray. I made a small incision about two inches above Minnie's navel. Then I attached a trocar to the end of a suction hose, turned the water on and began the process of removing gas, fluids and semisolids from the body cavities.

I punctured Minnie's lungs and stomach and aspirated their contents without incident. None of Minnie's internal organs had been removed because no autopsy had been performed. The doctor on call at the hospital when Minnie died had stuck with a safe assumption of 'natural causes' on the death certificate. I had moved on to her intestines when the trocar struck something substantial and the hose jerked and bucked at the encountered resistance. Surprised, I set the instrument aside. I wanted to take a closer look at what could be causing the obstruction.

I used a pair of forceps to hold the incision open and leaned in for a closer view. Something rapidly slid away from my touch, deeper into the small intestine. I jerked my head back and hit the overhead lamp, sending it swinging. I palmed the back of my head and grimaced, more out of surprise than real pain. Holly was staring at me and I felt my cheeks redden. Neither of us spoke. Something had slithered away from my forceps. It was dirty white, almost yellowish. And it was big. My mind formed a mental picture of an inflated condom, slick with mucus and unaccountably mobile. I was conscious of what I thought at first were scales. I realized I was panting.

I grabbed the scalpel from the tray and made another incision further down in the cadaver's lower intestine. In my zeal, it was more like a gash than an incision. The lining of Minnie's intestine opened to reveal the undulating yellowish form. It moved rapidly with spasmodic jerks. I heard Holly gasp but didn't look up.

Then it hit me: *tapeworm*. It had to be, though I'd never seen—or even heard of—a specimen that large. Not in length, but in girth. (I hope this isn't too upsetting Doctor Mayes. We could move on to other topics. No? Then with your permission, I'll continue.)

I used the forceps to grab the parasite and temporarily arrest its progress. It obviously sensed danger and twitched forward. Instinctively, I clenched my fingers in an attempt at holding the creature stationary. The tapeworm tore itself free from the forceps' grip I was left with several feet of inert segmented tissue. If you're surprised, don't be. This was nothing but the tail end.

Tapeworms are amazing creatures. For instance, a beef tapeworm has the capacity to grow between twenty and thirty feet long, but they're extremely slender. Think of those long balloons used to twist into balloon animals. Tapeworms are even thinner and more delicate. The one that lived inside Minnie was different. That one was, as I said earlier, much thicker. I used a condom as a reference and I stand by that description. The parasite's appearance was frankly astonishing. I am quite certain that the tapeworm ended Minnie's life. The idea of that gargantuan vampire sucking the life out of her from within is an appalling one, to say the least. No wonder her grandson said she 'ate like a horse.' The poor woman was trying desperately to survive!

I decided to try to contain the tapeworm and then contact the biology department at one of the local universities. Surely this specimen would be of particular biological interest.

"Help me flush it out."

"What the hell is it?" Holly asked. She didn't move.

"It's a tapeworm, an abnormally large one. If we can remove it intact, maybe we'll get our names in a medical journal or two."

"A tapeworm?" Holly repeated. She didn't sound convinced.

"Damn thing sucked her dry," I said. "No wonder she was skin and bones." Holly took a step closer, curiosity apparently getting the better of her. I was pondering my next move when the tapeworm made my ruminations unnecessary. It had reached the end of the line and, having nowhere else to go in its flight from my forceps, was now pushing its way out the cadaver's anus. I stared at the whitish knob-like head as it hung stationary for a moment and became aware of a shrill, girlish scream. I realized the sound was coming from me and shut my mouth. I felt my cheeks burning again as Holly's eyes darted between my face and the tapeworm, which was dangling close to the floor.

"Don't touch it, but don't let it get away either," I instructed her as I sped across the room to the utility closet. I realized I was contradicting myself, but I'm not great at thinking under pressure. I threw open the door and grabbed the mop and bucket we use to disinfect the floors. I discarded the mop itself, which landed with a clatter and kicked the bucket toward the cot. Holly stopped the rolling bucket with her hands, tipped it sideways and lowered one edge under the tapeworm's head right before it touched the floor. The creature continued to crawl from Minnie's cadaver into the bucket while Holly and I watched in horrified fascination. It was like watching dirty motor oil drain from an eighteen-wheeler; it just kept coming.

I realized we would need something to cover the top of the bucket so the specimen couldn't escape. I glanced around the room and, finding nothing that would suit my purposes, bolted for the stairs.

"Where are you going?" Holly called after me. I hollered back, "To find something to cover it with." Then I ran upstairs.

I raced around the building like a crazy person, but I had no luck in finding anything that I thought would safely contain such an enormous creature. I finally rushed back downstairs, intending to flip the bucket over and cover it with something heavy as a last resort.

I came back in the embalming room to find Holly kneeling on the floor, one hand covering her mouth in obvious dismay.

"What happened?" I asked.

Holly swallowed hard then squeaked, "It got away." She pointed down the drainage grate in the floor. "It was so aggressive, Bill! I tried to hold it in the bucket but..."

Several more feet from the tapeworm had broken off in the apparent struggle and lay inert in the bottom of the bucket. The head, along with a substantial portion of its body, had obviously fled to a more hospitable location. I shuddered inwardly as I imagined the tapeworm growing back to its original length—and perhaps longer—inside a new host.

I stepped forward and peered through the slits in the grate at the darkness below. I felt disappointed that the tapeworm had escaped. I was sure the interest in a partial specimen would be lukewarm at best. And I know the disappointment showed on my face because Holly practically looked sick, like she was afraid I blamed her.

"This is bad, this is really bad," I said, shaking my head solemnly. "Someday someone patrolling the sewers is going to find an anorexic alligator."

I gave Holly a broad grin then, to let her know it was okay. I hugged her since she still seemed pretty upset. I assured her that everything was fine and sent her home while I finished on Minnie myself.

Everything *was* fine, at least on the surface. But it was weird too, because I felt emasculated. Does that sound strange to you, Doctor? I was called upon to be the hero and felt like I came up short. I ran out of the room. I *wasn't there*.

Did Holly think that I chickened out and used finding a cover for the mop bucket as an excuse to run away? She assured me that she never thought that, but how can I know for sure? Maybe she was just sparing my feelings.

That night became a turning point for me.

I felt like less of a man around Holly, so I no longer flirted with her. I kept our talk focused on work. When she asked me why I was acting so cold toward her all of a sudden, I gave her a line about deciding it would be best if we kept our relationship professional.

Our lives continued for a little while under a cloud of unhappiness. It was as if everything in the world had faded somehow. The sky seemed gray even on sunny days but I stubbornly maintained my facade of indifference.

It didn't last, as you obviously can gather. After a month or two I noticed a change in Holly's appearance. She looked thinner and more physically fit. She started tanning. Not too much, but just enough. She got a cute new haircut and added a few really eye-catching pieces to her wardrobe. She looked more gorgeous than ever and she knew it.

I tried to deny my feelings; I really did. But then one day I entered the embalming room to find Holly wearing only a bra and panties and lying on one of the mortuary cots. The sight triggered a rush of memories and I just stood there flat-footed. My former lover gave me a knowing smile and slid so that her head hung over the edge of the cot. It was the position she had used to achieve such memorable results in happier times.

"We were so good for each other, Bill," Holly purred. "I miss you so much and I love you more than ever. I'll do anything to make this work. Look at my body Bill; isn't this what you want?" She arched her back and I threw in the towel.

So here we are. I'm engaged to the most gorgeous woman in the world. I agree with her when she says we're perfect for each other. I should be grinning from ear to ear and skipping around instead of moping over my predicament.

So here's where you can be of assistance. You are in a unique position, Doctor Mayes. You'll be able to examine Holly in close quarters. You'll be our patient, and she will be *yours*.

You see, there's something that's bothering me; something keeping me awake at night. Sex? Forget it. It's been like trying to play pool with a length of rope lately. Holly thinks its just nerves and that everything will be okay after the wedding. She's wrong. The problem I have—this mental stumbling block as you might refer to it—hinges on one question.

My extremely slender bride-to-be should be here momentarily to help me embalm you and prepare you for burial. Here, let me prop your eyes open. There we go. Holly will wash your body with disinfectant first and then we'll begin the arterial embalming. Was it the trailer of the big rig or the top of your convertible's windshield that beheaded you? It probably happened so fast that you aren't even sure. No matter. We can use your current state to our advantage; I'll position your head here on the end of the cot where you can observe the proceedings. We'll reattach your head later in the embalming process.

There should be enough time for you to make an assessment. Once you've seen her, Doctor Mayes, maybe you can help me decide something once and for all:

Did Holly swallow that tapeworm while I was gone?

TRANSFORMATIONS

Nicky only brought Derek along so she could reach the casket quicker.

For now, they dug side by side in the cool night air but soon she'd have to get rid of him. Nicky glanced at him. Derek's muscles flexed with each shovelful of moist earth he tossed aside. He worked tirelessly and methodically. She moved more sporadically, pausing to catch her breath every few minutes. Nicky knew Derek well enough to understand that he would never accuse her of not doing her fair share; he wanted her too badly to criticize. That was fine.

"Why don't you take a break?" he offered when he noticed Nicky leaning on her shovel.

Nicky hoisted her slender frame on to the edge of the hole, crossed her fishnet-clad legs and rummaged in her satchel for a cigarette. Derek stepped close enough to stand in front of her.

"Moon's bright tonight," he remarked. "It's perfect for grave robbing."

Nicky didn't respond.

"You know if you uncrossed your legs I bet it would give me incentive to work faster." Derek smirked as he ran a hand through his dyed-black hair and arched a pierced eyebrow.

"Not now," she said through a cloud of smoke, careful to keep her distaste from showing.

"You've been saying that ever since we met." The petulant brat rose up behind Derek's caustic Goth facade.

"Don't tick me off or you'll never get any."

Derek grumbled and he resumed digging.

BEDTIME STORIES FOR CARRION BEETLES

When Nicky's mother died, it was front page news. The headlines cruelly proclaimed the tragedy of rape, torture, and murder. Nicky survived by growing so numb inside, no feelings seemed to exist at all. Nicky's father descended into a mad delirium of self-loathing. The atrocities had been committed by a man, thus a potent self-hatred was born. Nicky's father judged himself guilty by association. The two of them barely acknowledged one another, both lost in their own coping mechanisms. It made for a fascinating home life.

Nicky gazed around the cemetery. The headstones seemed to glow in the moonlight. A warm breeze ruffled her hair. It was so peaceful. Maybe no one had to die tonight. But that was wishful thinking, because someone would die tonight, of that much Nicky was sure. She pushed her free hand into the fresh earth, savoring its coolness. Something moved against her palm. Nicky pinched it carefully and extracted a massive nightcrawler. She held it in her cupped palm. Nicky flicked her cigarette butt into the dirt pile and pressed her free thumbnail onto her palm, slicing the nightcrawler in half. Both ends writhed and thrashed until they spilled from her hand into the hole. Nicky dropped back in and stomped the halves to goo in a belated act of contrition.

Nicky shut out the world and rotted inside a pair of headphones. Father threw himself onto the roaring blaze of fervent lamentation and was burned beyond recognition. Where he found a whip for self-flagellation, Nicky never did find out.

Nicky's hands were beginning to blister, but she could not be deterred.

"I'm glad you picked a grave that's still fresh," Derek puffed as he hoisted his shovel. "The softer dirt makes for easier digging, thank God."

"There is no god," was Nicky's only response.

At five feet down they widened the hole, scraping dirt from the east wall of the hole. The hard dry earth here slowed their progress, but Nicky knew it was necessary. She'd need the room to maneuver when they reached the casket.

Nicky lay awake and listened to Father's guttural disgorge of guilt, shame and remorse. Nicky imagined the whip swinging furiously in high arcing motions over Father's shoulders like a frenzied demon. Nicky was astute enough to realize that Father punished himself for wrongs he'd committed toward his wife in their life together; wrongs both real and perceived. Nicky also knew that Father was punishing himself simply for being a man.

At a quarter past three, Derek's shovel blade struck metal. He knelt and used his hands to clear the last of the dirt clods from the top of the casket. It was a sectional with two lids. Nicky reached an arm over the lip of the hole and grabbed the cold blue steel handle of the .32 caliber pistol hidden in her bag.

Derek turned and grinned at Nicky. "Is this not the craziest thing you've ever done in your life?" He stepped forward and lowered voice. "You brought your digital camera right?"

"I brought this." Nicky lifted the .32 and pressed the end of the barrel against Derek's forehead.

One night soon after the beatings had begun, Nicky feigned sleep as Father stood in the doorway gazing at the bed. Father remained there for a long time. The next morning Nicky awoke to find the newly purchased miniskirt and halter top hanging from the closet door.

"Now be a good boy and pretend you're a statue," Nicky commanded. Derek's mouth hung open, his eyes widened. She almost felt sorry for him. "You are going to climb out of this hole. You are going to walk to your car and drive back to town. If you come back I will kill you. If you send the police I will kill you. If you do as I say, you'll never see me or have to worry about me ever again. Clear?"

Derek remained silent, seeming to formulate his reply. Finally the words tumbled from his mouth, "Nicky, I told you I'm cool with this. You said we'd dig up a corpse to see what it was like. I swear I won't tell. "

"I'll kill you if you say another word. I don't owe you any explanations, but I guarantee you do not want to see what happens next. Leave. Now."

Derek found a foothold and scrambled out of the hole. He staggered back a few steps, sprawled over a marker, then clambered back to his feet. Nicky followed him out of the hole to make sure he kept moving. He shot her one more disbelieving look, then spun on his heels and fled. Nicky watched him disappear into the darkness. She heard the distant rattle of keys and watched as Derek yanked the driver's side door open.

"You are one twisted bitch, Nicky!" Derek's voice cracked as he shouted. "I thought we'd made a connection but it turns out you're just some messed-up..." He paused long enough for Nicky to wonder if Derek was sneaking back toward her. Then the petulant brat was back in full force: "TEASE!"

Derek's last word echoed among the headstones as if the dead had taken up the accusation. Nicky waited and listened to Derek's roaring car engine fade away. She became aware of the crickets—boldest of the night creatures—as they resumed their song. Somewhere a night bird called. The breeze, cooler now, ruffled her hair again.

Father got a new job across the state line. They moved and the pair began a new life. The change worked wonders on Father's demeanor. His broken heart had apparently begun to mend at last. Father chatted with Nicky about the new school, new friends and new situations. Father spoiled Nicky with clothes, makeup and jewelry. Nicky pretended to be grateful because it made Father so happy.

Nicky tossed both shovels out of the hole and knelt on the bottom half of the sectional casket. The moon hung directly overhead like a spotlight shining on a solitary performer. Nicky felt with her fingers and found the seam between the upper lid and the side. She worked her fingers into the seam of the casket and pried, tentatively at first, then with more force. Two of her black press-on nails popped off. Cursing quietly, Nicky stood and rummaged in her satchel. She brought out a short crowbar and tried again. This time the lid popped up with surprising ease. Nicky started back, instinctively exhaling. The air surrounding her was a fetid miasma of expelled gases, flesh and formaldehyde. Nicky lifted the lid until it leaned against the east wall of the hole. Then she steeled herself, summoned an unbreakable resolve from deep within her and gazed down at the exposed corpse. Its face had twisted in a grimace as if, even now, the self-loathing overwhelmed any chance of peace.

"Hello Father," Nicky said.

Father passed away two days after Nicky's eighteenth birthday. The paramedics Nicky called were unable to revive him. Massive coronary, they said. Nicky was suddenly alone.

Nicky struggled to cope with feelings of resentment that were now growing at an alarming rate. Nicky felt afraid of unraveling the way Father had unless she followed through with her plan. She fumbled with the ribbon choker around her neck as she looked down upon her father.

"I'm afraid I'm not coping very well and we both know why." Nicky grabbed her satchel and pulled it down into the hole. She knelt and began to work quickly. First she lit two slender white candles and pressed them into the corners of the hole. The moon's glow had been sufficient for digging but she needed better lighting for what would come next. She laid out her arsenal on her father's motionless chest. With these weapons Nicky began to wage war against the demons of her recent past.

Nicky's fingers flew as she imposed her will on her father for the first time ever. "I know what you need," she muttered. Her fingers grasped a long pointed object and dragged the sharpened tip against both eyelids. She tossed the object aside. She used the contents of a stubby metal tube to make a garish crimson smear across his mouth. Nicky applied another compound until his cheekbones shone in a bruised shade of red. Then she brought out the metal tweezers. She pinched and yanked again and again. At last she straightened and surveyed her work.

"You look wonderful. It suits you, really."

She threw her weapons—eyeliner, lipstick, rouge and tweezers—back into her bag. Then she drew out a bouffant blond wig and lifted her father's head. Nicky's skin crawled at the unexpected watery creaking that his neck made but she kept a firm grip and fitted the wig on his head. Then it was time for the crushed red velvet gown. Nicky had used a razor to slit it completely down the back in preparation for this moment. She had it over her father's arms and tucked under his torso in two minutes.

Lastly, Nicky lowered her father's slacks and lifted the dress. His gray and withered member curled between his legs like the worm she had dispatched earlier. Nicky reached in her bag once more and fished out the garden shears. The blades wouldn't be very precise, but Nicky thought they'd be enough to do the job. She swallowed hard and willed her hands to move. Nicky angled the blades into position, closed her eyes and squeezed.

Snip.

Feeling a tad queasy, Nicky smoothed the dress back down, then stood and stretched the stiffness from her legs and neck. The breeze picked up. The candles flickered and her father's mouth seemed to twitch in a self-conscious smile.

"You still need a finishing touch," Nicky said, looking down. Her fingers automatically found the ribbon choker around her neck and she smiled. Nicky knelt once more and unclasped the choker. She tied it around her father's skinny neck. Her vision blurred with sudden tears. Nicky felt as if a great burden had been lifted.

All that remained was to close the casket on her transformed father, refill the hole and rebuild her life again. But it would be on Nicky's terms this time. Sobs wracked her exhausted frame.

"You coped and *you* survived only because I did what you wanted. You made it all about *you*. You forced your will on me because you were too afraid to change yourself. I love you and forgive you, but I need to take back what's mine."

A night bird cawed approval. The crickets sang their monotonous lullaby and the breeze buffeted Nicky's shoulder like a comforting pat on the back. Nicky's prominent Adam's apple bobbed as he sobbed, and his tears of anger became tears of relief.

#

The rescue mission thrift store was a drab cinder-block square.

The homely woman behind the counter was named Miriam, according to the tag pinned to her smock. Her jaw punished a piece of gum as she watched him stack the boxes on the counter.

"You sure you wanna donate all of this stuff?" Her fingers caressed the folds of a white silk blouse, then a black leather miniskirt. "This stuff is pretty nice; you could probably sell it or consign it somewhere."

"I just want to be rid of it all as quickly as possible."

"Oh, I see," Miriam said, though she obviously didn't. She lowered her voice. "Somebody pass away or something?"

"Those clothes belonged to someone my father liked having around," Nicholas replied. "But I never really got comfortable with her presence at all.

INCIDENT ON ALKALI ROAD

Lots of folks know somebody who acts a little crazy, but not many can say they know someone who's truly insane. I'm talking totally unhinged. The guy I'm thinking of was a little eccentric before. Now, thanks to me, he's been declared a 'danger to his self and others' and is currently a heavily sedated resident of Custer Sanitarium.

My name's Monte Durfee, by the way. The insane guy is Kent Norman. I know what you're asking: 'What the hell did you do to send this guy off the deep end?' It was an accident, I promise you that much. I didn't do any of it deliberately.

And what happened was pretty damned hard on me too.

It was hot as hell the day it happened. I'd driven my old Dodge east out of Sturgis on 34, windows rolled down, pedal to the floor. Had to be about ninety-five degrees and I figured my speed could match the temperature. I had plans to meet some friends in Rapid City for steaks and brews. About four miles north of Kent's place on Little Alkali Road the radiator on that piece of shit overheated. I steered into the ditch and decided to hoof it to his place. I don't own a cell phone and even if I did, the reception out there is more 'miss' than 'hit'.

The merciless bitch some call the sun beat down, browning the grass to a crisp. It didn't take long for my arms to redden and for my bald spot to burn. I wished I'd brought a hat.

BEDTIME STORIES FOR CARRION BEETLES

I spent a little over an hour shuffling down the gravel road that would eventually take me past Kent's farm. Not one damn vehicle passed. I wasn't really surprised though. Kent's people hadn't exactly settled on prime land. Finally, I crossed the road and hoisted a leg over the rusted strand of barbed wire that marked his property line. I cut through a row of scraggly jack pines on the west end of the farm—we call it a 'shelterbelt' because it's supposed to serve as a windbreak during the winter—and shambled toward the old house. Kent's father had apparently decided to let this particular field lie fallow before I was even born and I scrutinized the rusted skeletons of what I imagined was every car and truck the old man had ever owned. You could practically trace the evolution of the American automobile right there in that field.

I finally crunched over the gravel path that served as a driveway, past a broken refrigerator that stood sentry in the yard and mounted the steps to Kent's front door. I palmed sweat from my face and rapped on the door but no one responded. I pressed my forehead against the nearest rectangular window beside the door and peered inside. The only movement came from a few horseflies circling the air above the cluttered kitchen table. I kicked an empty beer can across the yard and looked in the ramshackle wooden shed where I thought Kent probably parked his truck. It was empty.

Would he mind if I went inside and helped myself to some water? It was hard to say. Kent's place wasn't my original destination, Rapid City was. We weren't exactly friends, either. We never really associated much at all. Kent might be a little pissed if I barged in without permission, but he'd get over it. At least I hoped so. Who'd be asshole enough to begrudge a thirsty man a drink of water? I tried the knob. The door was unlocked. I shoved it open, ducked inside and made a beeline for the kitchen sink. The inside of Kent's house wasn't as cool as I'd hoped, but the water was ice cold and fine as wine as far as I was concerned. I polished off two and a half glasses before I even thought to glance around.

Kent's a lifelong bachelor who'd taken to keeping to himself as much as he could. Not an overly friendly guy, if you get my drift. Kent stands about six foot three and weighs maybe two forty. It's all muscle. He has a big bushy gray beard, gaunt features and what I called 'coke-bottle glasses' when I was a kid. Not long ago Kent was a hell-raising biker. I could tell you some stories that would curl the hair on your head. He had this souped-up orange motorcycle that could drive up the side of a tree. Not all the way up, of course. What I mean is that he would steer his motorcycle up to the trunk of a big old elm tree, so that the front tire was just touching it. Then he'd rev the throttle just enough, and the motorcycle's front tire would shoot right up the side of the elm's trunk. Uncle Kent would be straddling that big orange monster grinning from ear to ear. Then he'd back it back down, nice and easy. I've seen pictures that prove it.

Then all of a sudden Kent, a guy who'd put more than two dozen guys on their backs in bar fights, wound up on his own. His back, I mean; he had a motorcycle accident.

Kent wasn't wearing a helmet—didn't even own one at the time—and could easily have died according to the doctors who treated him in the emergency room. Coming back from a wild night out, he'd wiped out on a patch of loose gravel and went sliding along on his face before cart-wheeling into the ditch. He spent a few weeks in the Meade County hospital. Should've been more, but the doctors couldn't convince him to stay. Most everyone in town thought he'd end up looking like the Phantom of the Opera or that comic super villain with half his face all scarred up.

We were all wrong. His face healed up rather nicely, and except for anosmia, which I found out is a fancy word for losing your sense of smell, Kent bears no physical scars from the accident. Emotional scars might be another story.

Kent didn't start wearing a helmet though. Instead, he stopped riding. Just drives a pickup now. Hell, he even buckles up. The booze even went away for a while.

From what I saw, Kent's life started to revolve around exercising and going to church. I thought church took place on Sunday mornings, but Kent went and found one that kept him busy not only every Sunday, but every Wednesday and Saturday night too. That's where he first met Gina Dowling. She became his 'lady friend' and that lasted for over two years.

One time, standing in line at the post office, I overheard a couple old bags saying that Kent had brought up the subject of marriage with Gina. She'd been reluctant and for reasons only she knew, had told him no. Kent took it mighty hard. Everyone could see it in his eyes and on his face whenever he came to town. Pretty soon after that Gina Dowling left town completely. Nobody saw her around. The general consensus was that she took the bus back home to her family though no one was sure where she was originally from. Either that or someone had come to get her. No one had seen or heard from her since. That was over a year ago.

How did Kent take her leaving? Nobody knew. Kent's not the type to share his feelings with anyone. Hell, he never even admitted that he'd asked her to marry him. So maybe he didn't care, but I never heard it brought up in conversations. Not with him. Kent still had enough of that ugly old temper to make folks not want to pry on a touchy subject. One thing though: Kent stopped going to church. That was the one place he associated most with Gina, so maybe that tells you something. Something else: Kent started drinking and brawling again.

What's that old country song? Something about time marching on, I think. That brings us back—or maybe forward—to me, standing in the middle of Kent Norman's kitchen.

Want to hear something crazy? I'd known him for over fifteen years but I hadn't ever been inside Kent's house. Not once. I got this giddy urge to start snooping around and it was too hard to fight.

A little cluster of breakfast dishes sat in the drying rack. A selection of magazines lay strewn across the kitchen table. Farming was the main topic of interest. I moved on. The floor boards squealed their protest as I walked, like they resented my being there. I peeked in the cupboards and found cups, dishes, old Tupperware. Kent had tucked a bottle of whiskey into the corner of the cabinet above the refrigerator. I resisted the urge to pour myself a shot or three.

Kent owned a television but it was covered with an old navy blue blanket. A tattered recliner hunched in one corner. Beside that stood a small end table, pockmarked with cigarette burns. A yellow lamp towered nearby. The air was stale, maybe a little gamy. I turned to face the nearest wall where several pictures hung. I was surprised to see Gina Dowling in most of them, even after everything that had happened. I stepped closer and noticed two things. The first was that even though everything else in Kent's home seemed to have the grimy look and feel of a lifetime of accumulated farm dust, the pictures of Gina were wiped clean. The second thing I noticed was that Gina wore the same frumpy green floral print dress in all the pictures. Did that woman own any other clothes? I snickered at her expense.

Following the narrow hallway brought me to the bathroom, which I only glanced in, then to Kent's bedroom. I could see countless dust motes floating in the beams of sunlight like inmates milling around a prison yard. It made me think of all of us living in our shitty little town and I suddenly felt restless and unhappy. A chest of drawers occupied one corner and opposite the foot of the bed double closet doors yawned open exposing a mishmash of flannel work shirts, denim coveralls, winter parkas and the like. Fly strips hung in all four corners. All of them were matted with black dots. Disgusted, I glanced at the bed and was seized by the hilarious notion that Kent had squirreled away a stroke magazine or two under his mattress. He was a lonely bachelor, after all. Next thing I knew, I'd stooped, intending to lift the mattress to sneak a peek. I was in this position when I heard the front door squeal open.

Guilt at being caught snooping gripped me. I was too far away to reach the bathroom, which would have been a plausible excuse for being inside Kent's house uninvited. I sure as hell couldn't casually say, "How ya doin' Kent! Just takin' the grand tour."

So I did what anyone in my predicament would do: I dropped to the floor and squirmed under the bed.

Kent plodded down the hall and straight into the bathroom. For a second I thought I could make a break for it, but the stream of piss sounded loud enough for me to realize he hadn't closed the door. Hell, living alone, he had no reason to. I waited.

Kent ambled back up the hall to the kitchen and I heard him fill a glass with water from the tap. Then he did the last thing I wanted him to: he came back into the bedroom and flopped onto the bed. I had a moment of claustrophobic panic as the box spring sagged toward me. Box springs shouldn't sag at all, but this one looked old and in desperate need of repair. Hell, I would've burned it and bought a new one. The trapped feeling gave way to another kind of fear as a strong urge to sneeze rose up from deep in my sinuses. I pinched my nose, pushing upward with my index finger and thumb. This was a trick I learned in school to avoid sneezing that I still use sometimes at the movies. The urge disappeared and I vowed to breathe through my mouth as long as I remained hidden there.

Kent tossed and turned a while, then began to sob. I felt a greasy sense of shame. I had violated Kent's privacy by snooping around his home, but I felt worse about violating the privacy of his feelings.

Sobs wracked Kent and it sounded like he was pounding the mattress with his fists. The situation was quickly becoming unbearable for me, lying wedged under his bed. I ground my teeth and clenched my own fists in frustration. I turned my head toward the far wall and my heart stopped.

Less than three feet away, past balled-up socks and bachelor-sized dust balls, lay a shriveled human corpse.

I jerked a hand to my face again, but this time, rather than pinch my nostrils shut to avoid sneezing, I chomped down on my hand to keep from screaming. I'm embarrassed to admit that I felt wet heat around my crotch. This coincided with the coppery taste of blood seeping into my mouth. I noticed no pain in my hand, though. I was too focused on the hideous grin and sunken black eye sockets of what once had been a face staring accusingly up at the box spring. I felt utterly revolted and my head swam. Then my mind took a little vacation.

I can't say how long I was out, but when I came to, my muscles were screaming in protest. My right arm felt numb from the bicep down because of how it was angled against my body. This turned out to be a blessing. When I tried to take my hand out of my mouth at first I couldn't move it. I opened my mouth wider and my palm limply fell free. Even in the waning light of the late afternoon, I could see that it was encrusted with dried blood. I'd really clamped down hard. I wondered how my teeth looked. Probably like a vampire's. Cutting off the circulation had obviously helped staunch any additional blood flow and had numbed the pain. Now that I had moved it, though, my hand began throbbing painfully and the length of my arm felt like it was grilling on a spit.

This'll sound crazy, but to take my mind off my discomfort, I looked again at the mummified skeleton. The remains appeared to be in the dry decay stage of decomposition. I saw only bone, wispy hair and the tattered remnants of a dress. Something about the dress tickled my brain. It was a floral print that could have been green at one time...

Oh sweet Jesus!

I realized it was Gina Dowling—or what was left of her. There wasn't a doubt in my mind. Kent must have hunted her down, or maybe she was dumb enough to come knocking on his door. I didn't know. What I did know was that Kent was one crazy and sadistic bastard for stuffing her body under his bed like this. Did he drag his souvenir out once in a while? Like maybe around bed time?

I realized I was shaking. I had broken out in a cold sweat fueled by revulsion and fear. The skeleton had now taken a back seat to my new terror: discovery and subsequent murder at the hands of a madman. If I felt the need to hide and keep silent before, those feelings were multiplied a hundredfold now.

Nausea swept over me and I closed my eyes. My hand throbbed angrily. I wanted to gag, thanks to the coppery taste in my mouth, and I longed for water. I thought I could easily drink a quart and still want more. Some of my muscles ached dully while others burned. I wondered if I'd even be able to move fast enough when the opportunity to escape arose.

Above me, I could hear Kent muttering in uneasy sleep. I knew his present location; that was something to be thankful for. I tried to wriggle my way out from under the bed but the floor below me creaked in protest and Kent snorted. I froze, acrid sweat burning my eyes, until his breathing became regular again. I didn't like how easily he'd woken so I resolved to stay where I was for the time being.

I looked again at my lifeless companion. Fate had brought us together and it was apparent that the situation would keep us that way, at least for a while. I had to make it a game to pass the time without losing my mind.

What did he do to you Gina? How did you die? I contemplated several grisly endings for Kent's former 'lady friend.' I heard the bed springs creak loudly as my uncle rolled closer to the wall.

To my astonishment, the wooden crossbeam nailed to the frame for support sagged downward significantly. Under the right side of the bed, the beam closed against my chest slightly, but under the left side, the board was now fully pressed against Gina's skull. The sight made me wonder if Kent had bashed her head in. I raised my right arm and tried to feel the back of the skull but couldn't get underneath it. Small tufts of brittle hair disintegrated at my touch. My middle finger pressed against a jagged crack and I followed it downward. I dislodged a bone fragment and felt it move away from my fingers and into the hollowed confines of the skull. I felt as if I was palming the most macabre piece of pottery in the world and pulled my hand away.

How long ago had Gina disappeared? *About a year ago.* What I still couldn't wrap my brain around was why Kent would hide her remains under his bed and let her rot right underneath him. I was convinced that she had decomposed *here*; the discoloration of the carpet and the abundance of dead bugs on the fly strips were evidence enough of that. Then realization hit me. It was the anosmia. After Kent's motorcycle accident he had lost his sense of smell. That was how he could stand it.

Hang up some fly strips and rest easy you crazy bastard! You've got anosmia, so what do you care?
uh-knows-mia... a-noose-me-yah... an-owes-me-a...

I mentally played with the word until I fell into a shallow doze. I dreamed.

A number of my family and friends were gathered around a table large enough to accommodate us all. As the various food dishes were passed from person to person, I noticed Gina sitting across from me. As I watched, her skin shriveled and darkened. Her eyeballs fell and dangled from their sockets. Gina's lips dried and receded. Her face contorted into a grimace. Everyone else continued to eat, ignoring her.

Then I realized Kent was sitting beside me, but not in a regular chair like the rest of us. He was sitting in an electric chair. Leather straps bound his feet, thighs, chest and arms. He stared forlornly at his plate. On his head perched the copper electrode helmet.

"You need to help get him out of that chair," a woman's voice said. She sounded tired and heartbroken. I jerked my head and was astonished to see Gina's skeletal jaw opening and closing in time with the words. The teeth only clicked and clattered, but in my mind I heard her final plea. "He doesn't belong there and you know it."

I jolted awake, smacked my forehead on the box spring frame and inhaled a cloud of dust mites and dead skin particles. A violent coughing fit swept over me. If Kent was still in the room I was a dead man.

I tensed up and listened. I heard water running. He was taking a shower. I threw a wary glance at the skull and the crossbeam. My dream came back to me and all at once I understood what had really happened. The knowledge broke my heart.

Before I could move, my old acquaintance padded back into his bedroom and sat down on the edge of the bed. From my vantage point, I watched him pull on faded jeans and a pair of gray athletic socks. I kept still and heard him remove a shirt from a hanger in the closet. I wasn't afraid of Kent anymore. Now I felt like I was protecting him. I heard him sigh as he left the bedroom. He paused to click off the bathroom light, and then shuffled to the living room. Silence spun out briefly until I heard his front door open and close. I waited for the muffled thump of the driver-side door to his pickup slamming shut. Then the pickup's engine roared to life.

I waited for the sounds of the vehicle to fade away and then began my long-awaited escape. My muscles screamed in protest as I wriggled free from my confinement. I shakily stood, tried to take a step and instead I flopped face first onto the bed. I gave myself a few minutes to build up some stamina and get the blood flowing again. When I tried standing a second time, my legs held, and after a couple tentative steps I began hobbling down the hallway, my good arm trailing the wall for support. I hadn't realized it lying on my back, but now that I was standing, I felt like my bladder was going to burst. I detoured into the bathroom and fumbled with my pants. I sprayed piss into Kent's pot for so long I started to get paranoid about him coming back for something and catching me midstream. After what seemed like minutes, I finished, flushed and crept back into the hallway.

By the time I reached the living room, I felt faint. I knew the emotional and physical tolls my mind and body had endured were working against me and the oppressive heat hadn't helped, either. I flopped into Kent's worn recliner, closed my eyes and waited for the fog to lift.

I jumped at a sudden sound. I lurched out of the recliner and tried to shake the cobwebs out of my head. The sound, I realized, came from someone approaching the front door. I stood flat-footed, trying to formulate a plan of action but coming up blank. The door flew open and I stood gaping foolishly at the face of Kent Norman.

"Monte Durfee?" He squinted at me and his breath reeked of whiskey. "What the hell you doin' in my home?"

I couldn't think of a damned thing to say.

Kent leaned toward me, scowling. The smell of single malt nearly singed my nose hairs. He was tore up. How long had I been out?

"You tryin' to steal from me? That it?"

I shook my head in denial but he shot one big paw out and grabbed my shirt. Before I could say a word, Kent slammed his other fist into my face. A nauseating crunch exploded in my ears as the cartilage in my nose collapsed. Hot blood sprayed in every direction.

"Don't you ever steal from me, you little weasel!"

My eyes streamed tears and the room blurred. Kent swung again and something like white fireworks exploded inside my eyes. I raised my arms in a feeble attempt at covering my face, but it was useless. Kent hit me three more times in rapid succession. My knees buckled and I would have fallen if Kent had let go of my shirt.

"Any last words, thief?" Kent growled.

"Please just stop…let me explain!" I was sure that in his rage he would keep pounding me, not stopping until I was dead. I thought of the corpse under his bed and said the only thing I could think of to get him off me: "Gina's…in there…under your bed."

I pointed feebly. Kent froze, one fist still clenching my shirt, the other cocked in midair. His mouth hung open and his eyes widened. He must have decided I was telling the truth, although he couldn't understand what I really meant. He relaxed his grip on my shirt and I dropped like a rag doll onto the dusty carpet. Kent's pounding footsteps receded and everything in my world faded to black.

* * *

Sheriff Ryan Salazar was waiting in my hospital room for the moment I woke up. He had a few answers and a lot of questions. I helped him out as best I could, by telling the truth about why I'd been in Kent's house in the first place and explaining the sagging box spring and the loose board. I told them what I thought had happened and the sheriff seemed to agree.

A couple days later, after I got released and had healed up some, I downed a few cold ones with Deputy Eddie Johnson at Gunsey's Bar. He knew less than the sheriff, but was able to speculate more, being off duty and all. We think we have a pretty good idea what happened.

After the rejected marriage proposal, Kent and Gina had parted on bad terms. Then Gina had sneaked into Kent's house. Maybe she changed her mind or came to apologize. If Kent wasn't there and she started snooping around, she'd probably found herself in a position very similar to mine: overwhelming panic at being caught somewhere she wasn't supposed to be. So she did exactly what I had done; she hid under the bed. That tells me she wasn't coming back on good terms, or she would have crawled *into* the bed. What's so tragic and obscene is she happened to be lying right under the part of the box spring that had the tendency to sag the most. Kent came into his room—all six foot three, two hundred forty pounds of him—and flopped down on that part of the bed and crushed her skull. Gina must have died instantly and Kent never even knew it.

How did Gina get to his farm without getting noticed? Don't know. It's possible she hitched a ride with someone. It could have been someone from Rapid City or Spearfish who never even knew who she was or that everyone thought she'd left town. Maybe they heard but kept their mouth shut, not wanting to get involved. Or she could've just walked. Gina never did own a car, as far as Eddie or I knew. But when she disappeared, most everyone in town just figured she hopped on the bus and went away. Eddie says Sheriff Salazar might be in hot water for not investigating.

When Kent dropped me and went searching for Gina, he didn't have to go far. I'd told him right where to look. It's not hard to imagine him coming unhinged when he found her. His lost love had been there all along, rotting under his bed. I shudder every time I think about it.

Sheriff Salazar is the one who actually pulled into Kent's driveway. He did it just in time to see a chair come flying out a side window. The sheriff was looking for me, believe it or not. When I never showed up in Rapid City and no one could get hold of me, one of my buddies called it in. Thank God I had more friends than Gina Dowling apparently did. Sheriff Salazar found my truck in the ditch and stopped at the next farm: Kent's.

Based on the condition of the house when the sheriff finally arrived, Kent must've gone completely apeshit. He tore the place apart, literally. Eddie says I'm damn lucky to be alive. Thinks Kent must've forgotten about me lying there on the floor.

The sheriff couldn't get Kent to calm down at all. Instead, Kent came after the sheriff when he saw him. Salazar had to put two slugs from his old Colt .45 slab side into one of Kent's knees just to get him to go down. Even then Kent kept coming. Eddie said when he got the radio call for backup, Sheriff Salazar told him to bring a tranquilizer gun.

So that's the series of events that led Kent Norman to be deemed a threat to his self and others and why now he spends his time under sedation at Custer Sanitarium. And now you know why, technically, it's my fault. I like to think, that by explaining what I'd seen under Kent's bed, I saved him from the electric chair. I don't pat myself on the shoulder too much, though.

These days, I'm prone to crying fits and I can never seem to drink enough. I'm not talking about water. I have a lot of trouble sleeping in my bed now too. I have to fight the urge to check under it every few minutes. I usually drift off in my recliner instead. Sometimes I dream.

In my dreams, friends, family and folks from town are gathered around a big dinner table. This time the seat across from me—the one Gina had occupied—is empty. Maybe that means she's at rest.

Kent is still beside me in the dream, but instead of being strapped to an electric chair, he's bound up in a straitjacket. He thrashes in his chair, groaning and gibbering while the rest of us eat, but at least he's still alive and at the table. That's something to be thankful for.

Isn't it?

THE RED PATCH IN THE SNOW

The red patch in the snow got into his head.

Gabriel Dawson stood at the window and gazed out at the white expanse of strange formations and mysterious outcroppings that winter had transformed his back yard into. Naked shrubs hunched like skeletal hens nesting in defiance of the bitter wind. Clouds of snowflakes twisted and capered in the frigid air like Nordic demons on holiday. And there was the red patch to consider. Gabe squinted and tried to identify the object that seemed to nestle in the ever-shifting white banks. *A piece of trash? A child's red mitten or half-hidden scarf?* Gabe couldn't quite decide.

The winter chill outside matched the emotional temperature of the room. Gabe and Alyssa had argued twenty minutes before. Something had happened at work that had reminded his wife of some past misdeed Gabe himself had committed. She had swept into the room ready for battle, needing to revisit old grievances. Gabe believed that time should heal all wounds and had little patience for digging up hatchets that were better left buried. But Alyssa had an ax to grind, if one can be forgiven for such an egregious mixing of metaphors, and in minutes, the couple had nearly been at each others' throats physically, while emotionally they were a thousand miles apart.

Gabe sighed. He thought about Alyssa. His imagination shook free from the leash of logic and bounded ahead into dangerous territory. *Where was she? Who was she with?* Gabe's mind created scenarios of betrayal and revenge being committed against him. He clenched his fists in frustration and fought the lump setting up camp in his throat, a victim of his own morbid imagination. As tears blurred his vision, he reached for the whiskey bottle hidden in the bottom drawer of his desk. He skipped the formality of a glass. As he tried to drown his fears, he noticed again the red patch out in the snow.

Forty-five minutes later, he emptied the bottle and, like a child returning to a cupboard in search of nonexistent treats, Gabe felt around in his desk drawer again. His fingers found no miraculous second bottle but instead closed around his chamois-wrapped handgun. It was a Glock 22 purchased "for protection". Gabe idly jacked the clip out, checked it and slammed the clip home. As he did this he listened to the goading whisper of snow against the window pane. Every time he glanced outside his eyes sought out the red patch. *A scarf; it has to be.* The sound of tires crunching snow shifted Gabe's attention back to his own inner turmoil.

Alyssa burst into the house and brought the winter with her. She eyed him frostily as she unzipped her parka.

"Where have you been?" Gabe held the Glock out of view behind his hip. Alyssa curled her lip defiantly. Gabe trembled a little; she was more beautiful with her face twisted in a scowl than most women were when they smiled.

"I just want to know where you ran off too." Gabe fought to stay calm. "Seems like every little thing sets you off lately."

"I'm tired of your drinking, Gabe. Absolutely sick to death of it, in fact."

"Come on, everybody has their vices."

"Well I think that's just super, Gabe," Alyssa retorted with brittle politeness. "So what if I told you *my* vice is hooking up with Chuck from your work?"

Gabe remembered the pang of jealousy he'd felt as Alyssa giggled at all of Chuck's jokes at the office Christmas party. Now an image of the pair entangled in bed sheets assailed his mind. He mentally crumpled up the image and tossed it aside but the next image that popped into his brain lacked the protective buffer of the bed sheet. Gabe groaned aloud.

"Hey, everybody has their vices." Alyssa gave an exaggerated shrug and held out her hands as if to say, *nothing you can do about it now, is there?*

Gabe flipped off the safety, raised the gun, and shot her in the face. All the X-rated scenes in his mind turned into snuff porn. Suddenly nauseated, Gabe fled the house and stumbled into the back yard, his heart pounding. Right or wrong, he'd made his choice. The idea that she'd been lying to emphasize a point suddenly occurred to him. The realization came twenty seconds too late.

Where's it at? Gabe felt an overwhelming desire to find the red patch in the snow. There was safety in this mundane endeavor. Everything else could wait; right now he needed to satisfy his curiosity. The winter wind howled in his face and blasted him with icy throwing-stars, but he gritted his teeth and kept scanning the ground.

Much to his chagrin, the mysterious red patch that had gotten into his head was nowhere to be found. Gabe squinted in the approaching dusk but saw nothing out of the ordinary. Sure that he now stood exactly where he'd seen the splash of color from his window, he paused and gazed back at the house. Inside, he knew Alyssa lay in a growing puddle of dark crimson. Out here, Gabe was surrounded by arctic white. So where was the red patch in the snow?

Gabe glanced down at the gun and realized the truth of what he'd been looking at all afternoon. Could something tragic echo backwards through time? Could an object leave an afterimage before it even happened? Gabe raised the Glock and mashed the barrel into one nostril. He pulled the trigger and completed his own self-fulfilling prophecy.

The red patch in the snow came out of his head.

THE RESTORATION ROOM

Once a person gets used to the smell they're no bother at all.

But then, I've never been a woman who's asked for much. Four walls and a roof over my head, food enough to eat, water enough to drink and some clothes to wear; that's all I ask. Most southern belles want a lot more than that, but not me. I have the love of a good woman and the essentials. What more do I need? I ask for no money, weapons, trinkets or the like, but Lord how that stuff piled up around us! I wonder if the soldiers will take it all with them when they leave. *If* they leave.

* * *

The wilderness of Spotsylvania County seemed like the perfect spot for Rowena and I to make our home. We braved the impenetrable growth and rough terrain and chose a place to homestead several miles from tiny Chancellorsville. We slept in an improvised lean-to against the side of a ravine until Rowena discovered the cave. I remember how excited she was when she first told me about it.

"Lizzie! Come look!" Her hair had come undone and she looked beautiful and childlike in the sun.

"Rowena, what on earth has gotten into you?" I wondered aloud.

She grabbed my hands and led me about forty yards from where we'd set up camp.

"Look! A little cave," Rowena beamed. "We can sleep here while we build our cabin."

I crawled into the cave and had a brief look around. It was small but with enough space that we could both sleep comfortably inside. The cool interior gave me another idea. I proposed that we incorporate the little cave into our home. If we built the cabin flush against the ravine, we could use the cave as a natural root cellar for canned goods and supplies. Rowena loved the idea and when all was said and done, that's just what we did.

As the walls of the cabin rose up slowly but surely, I also found time to plant a garden to see us through that first winter. Rowena did the hunting; I never could quite bring myself to pull the trigger on an animal.

We celebrated our one year anniversary with stewed rabbit, carrots and tomatoes, sitting at the small hand-carved wooden table in the center of our own home.

Our happiness seemed limitless. We didn't know that in less than a month, bloody war would break out. Despite its eventual name, it proved to be anything but civil.

We learned about the War Between the States on our sojourns into town and from the occasional traveler. It seemed a shame that we couldn't resolve our differences with the Yankees peaceably. I guess their self-righteous fingers pointing in our direction got to be too much to bear.

At the end of April in '63 Rowena came running up to the cabin looking like someone had just spit on her mamma's grave.

"Lizzie! Get inside and stay there!" She grabbed at my hands. I pulled them away because my fingers were dirty from pulling weeds in the garden.

"What's wrong?" I asked as I wiped my hands on my apron.

"The Federals are concentrating their forces near Chancelorsville," Rowena paused and gasped for breath. I found myself admiring the pretty flush of her cheeks. "Lee's Army of Northern Virginia is going to drive them back. I want you here at home where I can protect you."

We didn't need any protecting from the battle itself, but later it seemed as if the battlefield had been picked up and moved to our front yard. I'd never seen so much blood and gore.

We heard the riders before we saw them.

Through the scrub brush we caught glimpses of three mounted riders. There were two Confederate soldiers and an old colored fellow who rode between them. Rowena and I stood just outside our door and waited for their arrival.

"Afternoon, ladies." The lead rider, a tall sunburnt blond, doffed his braided hat and bowed after he'd dismounted. "I am 1st Lieutenant Bell and this is Corporal Johnston." He motioned toward his fellow soldier, a muscular young man with a thick neck and bristling eyebrows. No one introduced the colored man.

Rowena and I both murmured our hellos and I started to curtsy but got an elbow in my side before I could complete the gesture. I straightened and cast a sidelong glance at Rowena, whose lips were drawn in a tight white line.

"We've a bit of food and a bit of firewood, but not much on hand for you to beg, borrow or steal," she told the lieutenant.

The corporal stiffened and began to growl in reply but Bell smiled amiably and approached. He came forward until he stood directly before us. The lieutenant leaned so close I could see a stray eyelash perched on his sunburned cheek. The brass buttons on his tunic gleamed in the sun.

"You ladies may be near something that could be a tremendous asset to the Confederacy in our righteous battle against the Federal invaders. Corporal Johnston and I are operating independently within the Confederate States Army under the command of General Thomas J. Jackson." Bell paused, probably to make sure we recognized the name, and went on. "Stonewall has given us a vital mission. We'll be examining the side of this ravine for a certain cave that may prove to be of great significance."

I confess I started at this information but Rowena kept her composure. "You must do as you see fit, Lieutenant."

Bell turned and motioned for the corporal to bring the old colored man forward. Johnston roughly hauled their prisoner toward us. I realized the man's wrists were shackled.

"Old Zeke here has an unusual talent," Bell announced. I noted a lonely thread of admiration woven through the tapestry of hatred and contempt the young officer obviously held for the old man.

He now stood before us and I saw that a milky film covered his eyes, making them match his cotton-white curls.

"Though he's blind as a bat, old Zeke will lead us to a special place said to contain potent magic that we shall harness for the good of the Confederacy."

The old man bowed deeply and began to speak. "Ezekiel Walker. I am humbled—"

"Nobody said you could talk," Corporal Johnston growled and jammed the butt of his rifle into the colored fellow's kidneys. The old man's knees buckled and he toppled with a groan. Rowena's hand found mine and squeezed it tightly. Ezekiel stayed curled in the dirt until the soldiers hoisted him to his feet.

"Focus on the job at hand, old man," Bell instructed. "Now tell us. Where do we start?"

Ezekiel steadied himself and breathed a few deep breaths. Then his shoulders slumped. "I have found the Special Place already. It is very close." The old fellow pointed a gnarled finger in the direction of our cabin. Rowena and I exchanged puzzled glances.

"You better be sure, Zeke," the lieutenant warned. When Ezekiel nodded, Bell turned back to us. "Did you build your cabin flush against the ravine wall?"

"Yes." We responded simultaneously without meaning to.

"We'll have to tear it down," Bell announced.

I began to protest but Rowena held up a hand. "Lieutenant, may I ask Ezekiel a question?"

"Make it quick."

"Mr. Ezekiel, is this 'Secret Place' you seek a small cave?"

The colored fellow paused to consider the question. Then he replied quietly, "It could be a cave, yes. But if the legends are true then it is not small."

"What is the significance of this place?" Rowena asked.

"That's enough." Lieutenant Bell spoke up before Ezekiel could answer. "Allow us inside to examine your home or we'll have to resort to the use of force."

"Force will not be necessary," Rowena replied a bit tartly. It seemed to me that she'd taken an instant dislike to the two soldiers. I didn't blame her a bit. Were we about to lose our home, built with our own sweat and toil, in order to aid the war effort?

Our little procession marched into the cabin. Rowena led the way and pointed at the door to our makeshift root cellar. "I believe that is what you men are seeking."

Bell and Johnston anxiously moved forward. "This ain't it," Johnston growled once he'd opened the little square door. "Not enough space in there."

The corporal spun toward the old man and I thought he was going to beat him. But it was Bell who sidled up to Ezekiel. "Now, Zeke, you wouldn't be trying to make a fool out of me, would you?"

The colored man shook his head emphatically.

"Then what are we doing here, Zeke? You know I won't be very happy with you if we waste any more time. Stonewall's waitin' on you, boy."

Ezekiel's sightless eyes wandered again toward our natural root cellar. "I can't understand it. It's right there. It's enormous. I can see it."

Corporal Johnston had apparently had enough. "See it? You can't see a damn thing you lying—"

"Wait!" Rowena shouted as she stepped forward. "Maybe there's more to the cave than first meets the eye."

The soldiers looked at her and then at each other. Lt. Bell instructed me to furnish him with a lit oil lantern. After I did this, Corporal Johnston crawled into the cool interior of the cave through the square door we'd built.

Bell handed the lantern in to Johnston. "What do you see, Corporal?"

"Just jars of food. Wait a moment..." Johnston handed out a jar of snap beans that I'd canned a few weeks earlier. I stepped forward and took it from him. Rowena grabbed two jars of stewed tomatoes from his out-thrust hands. We hurried to our dining table with the jars. Ezekiel stood near the door and remained silent. The corporal sent out several more jars which we carried to the table.

"I think I've found something, Lieutenant!" The corporal's disembodied voice called. He clambered back out of the cave and brushed his uniform perfunctorily. "There's a hole, no bigger than a five-cent piece, but it is right in the middle of the far wall. I bet we can widen the hole and see what's on the other side."

"Good work, Corporal," Bell responded and turned to where Rowena and I stood. "Do you have a pickax or anything we could use to break the rock?"

We didn't and said as much.

"We'll have to make due with our bayonets," The lieutenant said. He sent Corporal Johnston out to retrieve them.

"Why so gloomy, old man?" Bell asked Ezekiel, who only hung his head in response. "Chin up, Zeke, you've done your job and soon you'll be going home."

The old man murmured something so quietly I couldn't hear. At that moment Johnston burst back in carrying two rifles with the bayonets secured to their barrels. Bell's next words sent a shiver down my spine:

"For the glory of the Confederacy, let us open our secret weapon."

The pair took turns widening the minuscule hole in the back of the cave with their bayonets until they had created a gap large enough for a man to squeeze through.

Then Lt. Bell beckoned us outside. Rowena and I stood together to one side of our door. Corporal Johnston stood next to Ezekiel on the other. The lieutenant paced in front of us.

"Your cabin is being appropriated for use by the Confederacy. Soldiers from the Confederate States Army will come here to recover from their wounds. If you wish to maintain residence in the cabin, you will be permitted to do so as long as you perform the following duties." Lt. Bell paused and I almost thought Rowena was going to challenge him but she kept her peace.

"You will cook for any of the men who are able to eat. You will keep their packs and their belongings until the men are well enough to return to battle. You will allow free and constant access to the cave we've opened up. If a wagon arrives in the dead of night, you will let the soldiers in." The lieutenant had stopped in front of Ezekiel and his lips twitched as he seemed to be holding back a smile. "And one more thing," he added. "You can give Zeke a proper burial if you think he deserves it."

He shoved his bent and battered bayonet into the old man's chest and twisted the blade. Ezekiel tried to speak but instead began drooling blood. Corporal Johnston stayed behind him and made sure he remained impaled.

The Lieutenant gritted his teeth with effort and lifted the old man a few inches off the ground. Ezekiel's feet jittered and kicked and he feebly grabbed for the barrel of the gun. I began to feel faint and staggered backward until I half fell against the wall of our cabin and slid to the ground. I bent my head between my knees to keep from passing out and was only dimly aware of the soldiers mounting their horses and riding away through the brush.

I heard Rowena murmuring as if from far away. A wet, rasping voice answered. The poor fellow still lived. As one who would rather can vegetables than hunt rabbits, this current development felt to me like a waking nightmare. Rowena continued her mutterings for a few minutes more and then stood.

The figure that turned to face me was still the woman I loved, but what a ghastly change had taken place! Her hands, arms and dress were drenched in dark, rapidly coagulating blood. I looked up at her face in astonishment. Tears crawled down her cheeks through the blood like rivulets of honey.

The eyes that stared past me were milky white and sightless.

I lay abed, still recovering from a fever brought on by shock when the first wounded soldiers arrived.

How Rowena managed to bury the old man, nurse me, and cope with her own condition is something I'll never fully understand. Though she no longer had her sight, Rowena moved with grace and assurance. She almost seemed angelic.

Confederate and Federal forces fought what became known as the battle of Chancellorsville so close to our cabin that we could hear the sounds of the bloody battle echoing across the hills. By talking to the brawny driver of the first wagon we learned that General Robert E. Lee's Confederate Army of Northern Virginia had suffered heavy losses.

The driver pounded on our door one overcast afternoon and when Rowena opened it, the soldier just stood there awkwardly wringing his hat in his hands. He never even introduced himself as far as I remember. "I'd better get to it," he said and returned to his wagon. I rose and joined Rowena at the door.

"I'd be obliged if one of you ladies would open the door to the Restoration Room while I unload," the soldier hollered when he noticed us still standing there. *The Restoration Room?* Is that what they'd taken to calling it? I let that go for the moment as I squinted in the direction of the wagon. I'd stayed indoors for so long that the sun made the scene almost too bright to look at and my eyes throbbed painfully in their sockets.

I could see the wounded soldiers lying in the back of the wagon. Seemed to be quite a few of them packed in like cord wood. The brawny fellow who'd come to the door was the only one who seemed to be moving. He plodded to the back of the wagon and grabbed one of the wounded men by the ankles and pulled. The injured soldier slid from the top of the pile and thudded to the ground. The wagon driver dragged him through the brush and past our tomato plants. The wounded man's hand waved and pointed as if indicating which tomatoes were ripe enough for picking.

Looking at the garden, I realized two things simultaneously. First, Rowena has also managed to somehow tend to our garden while I'd been ill and second, the men in the wagon were not injured, but dead.

The brawny soldier dragged the corpse of his comrade in through our front door, across our floor and then dropped his legs and straightened, panting slightly. He turned and handed me a bag which I realized was the dead soldier's haversack, probably filled with the usual set of eating implements, canteen and perhaps even a frying pan.

"He won't need this in there, but if what I've heard is true, he'll need it when he comes back out." I stood there gaping at the man, completely flabbergasted. He knelt and hefted his comrade's body through the door to the part of the cave that had served as our root cellar. Then he crawled in after it. The brawny fellow repeated the process as he pushed the dead man through the hole in the wall of the cave. For some reason I thought of bees in a hive.

He emerged from the outer cave and trudged back out the front door. Our first visitor spent the next hour dragging bloody corpses across our floor and stuffing them into the hole in the wall. Each time he entrusted to me the dead soldier's haversacks and, in some cases, other personal belongings as well. A shaving kit, a Bible and other items grew into a pile on our table.

After the last body had been carried in and disposed of, the soldier turned to us and bowed. He was panting, soaked with sweat and his face looked ashen.

"Sorry for the intrusion." He glanced at our blood-smeared floor and added, "I'm sorry about the awful mess."

Then he stepped outside and, before returning to his wagon, vomited violently among the tomato plants.

Other wagons followed the first. We learned that only soldiers with intact heads were candidates for the 'Restoration Room.' Soldiers who'd lost a leg or arm were also deemed unfit. "They need to be able to see, march and shoot," was how one soldier unloading corpses explained it.

Things got so that I'd no sooner finish scrubbing the floor and a new group would arrive. The wagons were now tended by two soldiers but the task was still a gruesome and physically demanding one for all who undertook it.

I picked up details about the battles and the progress of the war by chatting with the soldiers and listening in when they spoke amongst themselves. All the dead came from the Battle of Chancellorsville initially, but over the course of a year, our cabin saw hundreds upon hundreds of dead soldiers interred in the 'Restoration

Room'. Every time the arrivals started to taper off, a sudden influx of new bodies threatened to overwhelm us.

"Bloody fighting a few miles from the Orange Turnpike," one wagon driver revealed about thirteen months after the first shipment. "Ewell's and Hill's corps are getting slaughtered out there. Now Longstreet's got himself shot. How long does that goddamn cave take to work anyhow?"

One of the soldiers the complaining fellow unloaded that day was our old acquaintance Lt. Bell. For some reason, recognizing his face amidst all the other corpses gave me quite a turn. The steady procession of dead had numbed me, but seeing someone who had been alive the last time he entered our cabin reaffirmed the terrible toll the war was taking.

Another soldier a few days later shook his head and muttered about a battle happening near the Spotsylvania Courthouse. The procession of corpses from this battle lasted for weeks.

Rowena accepted it all with Southern grace. I confess that my blond locks had all but turned white from the strain of this ghastly business. Time and time again I implored Rowena to let me pack our belongings so we could flee. Rowena steadfastly refused. "My place is here now, Lizzie," she told me on more than one occasion. "Guarding the cave is my lot in life, whether I like it or not." I had no idea then what she meant.

I did notice that each soldier who completed his grisly task always reemerged from our old root cellar looking haunted and haggard. Not that I could blame them. But after a while, I began to suspect the living soldiers were enduring something even more terrifying than the job of piling their casualties in a cavern under a misguided notion that the place somehow held mystical healing powers.

One night in early spring of 1865, I worked up the courage to take a closer look at the hole in the cave wall. We'd long since stopped using the area as a root cellar and except for cleaning up after each delivery, I never strayed too close to the square door. That night, I waited for the sound of Rowena's breathing to ease into deep regularity and then I slipped from beneath the covers and padded toward the cave. I pulled the door open and felt my pulse racing as I clambered into the antechamber. One of the still-living soldiers had pounded a spike into the wall and had hung a lantern there. I felt for it in the dimness and lifted it down. I found the box of phosphorus matches I'd secreted away in the pocket of my nightgown and lit the lantern. Fighting an almost overwhelming sense of trepidation I leaned forward and extended the lantern so that a feeble ray of light illuminated the first few yards of the cavern's interior.

Never in my life have I witnessed such a macabre scene. And coming from me, that should speak volumes. The cavern was indeed much larger than anyone realized. I'd believed that the corpses were being dropped into a bottomless pit, but it seemed that the available space extended horizontally rather than vertically. In the scant seconds that I gazed into the cavern, my eyes fell on rows upon rows of soldiers. Not dead, yet not living. Bloody wounds had crusted over but not healed. The pallor of every figure inside the cavern was a ghastly gray that matched their tunics and trousers. The gold buttons on the tunics reflected the lantern light but their dark eyes did not. That might have been the single most appalling detail of the entire scene.

Shine a lantern light at an animal prowling in darkness and their eyes will reflect the light in all manner of startling colors. But the dead eyes of these soldiers reflected nothing. It was as if their eyes were instead reflecting the eternal darkness of their current home—and of their souls.

My mind scrambled and tried to come up with the number of bodies I'd seen pushed through the hole in the wall over the last two years. My brain rejected the number. Thousands of casualties were officially reported missing. Thousands of silent gray figures hunched inside the cavern practically within our home. Rowena and I had made our bed twenty feet from a veritable army of the undead. The constant creaking sounds told me that the soldiers had the ability to move, but they all seemed content to sit as if patiently awaiting orders. I wondered where in the cavern's expanse Lt. Bell sat and visualized him suddenly jumping up and lunging at me in recognition.

Unable to bear the sight of the soldiers any longer, I hurriedly extinguished the lantern and scrambled from the empty former root cellar. I scraped my shins on the way out and slammed the square door behind me. I felt the overwhelming urge to seal it more securely but there was no lock—and never had been.

I shrank back from the door and shrieked aloud when Rowena softly spoke my name. I stumbled back to our bed and tumbled onto her lap. Rowena stroked my hair and murmured to soothe me as I sobbed.

Eventually I recovered my senses enough to begin asking questions.

"Are they alive?"

"To a certain degree, yes. The cave does have limited 'restorative powers' as Lt. Bell said."

"How can that be?"

"I do not know for certain. Neither did Ezekiel. He believed—as do I—that some residue leftover from a being who sojourned here long ago is the cause."

"But what's keeping them from pouring out and rejoining the war?" I shivered as I considered a battle against an army of soldiers who couldn't be killed.

"I am." Rowena said this so quietly that it almost didn't register with me. I turned my head and looked up into her eyes. Though still milky and sightless, they seemed to see so much more than mine.

"Did you say—?"

"Yes, Lizzie. I know the sacred incantation that keeps them all trapped inside the cavern. It is my duty to keep them hidden away where they cannot add to the bloodshed."

"But how?"

"Ezekiel revealed the incantation to me. He spoke the words in my ear and gave me instructions with his dying breaths. I grew up with some colored folks living close by, and they were always just as sweet as peach pie to me. I never agreed with this godforsaken war. I wanted to help, and I think Ezekiel could sense that. When his spirit passed on, he bestowed his gifts upon me."

"Gifts!? You went blind!"

"It is a heavy burden that I carry."

"Then share it with me! Teach me the words that keep the undead from leaving the cavern."

"Hush, my love. I don't want you to suffer the same fate. You always looked at the world with the wonder and innocence of a child. Someday, you will again. Someone else will come along, and when the time is right, I'll share the incantation with them. Now, we both need our rest, so sleep."

And wonder of all wonders, I did.

BEDTIME STORIES FOR CARRION BEETLES

The wagon-loads of fallen soldiers trickled and became the exception rather than the rule. It seemed fewer and fewer soldiers remembered or knew of this place. In May of 1865 we received word that Lee had surrendered at Appomattox.

* * *

That was decades ago. Rowena and I stayed and did our best to make the cabin feel like our home again. But once a month she'd slip away and crawl into the old root cellar and renew the incantation. She always promised that she'd share her knowledge with the right person when he or she came along, but insisted that the next guardian would be a stranger to us. Rowena said wanted to spare me the burden and would never relent.

Now I fear that the window of opportunity has closed. Rowena got bit by a snake and now she's bedridden with fever. My love raves and mutters her way through fever-induced nightmares. My heart is breaking because it seems like she's fighting a losing battle. Rowena is so frail now I'm afraid of what a wagon journey might do to her. I'd ride into town alone, but am afraid to leave her side should she awaken and be ready at last to tell me what I need to know.

If only a traveler would happen by! But visitors are all but nonexistent these days. We have grown old and the world has moved on without us.

I am afraid of two things.

I am afraid of losing the love of my life; the woman who sacrificed so much of herself to do what she felt was right. My admiration of Rowena is as deep as the ocean.

As for my other fear, that should be obvious. I am afraid that Rowena will never recover sufficiently enough to tell me how to keep the passage sealed. If Rowena passes and the incantation is not renewed when it should be, how soon before the lost souls within the cavern grow restless? How soon before an army of the undead spews forth and runs rampant across the land?

I'm holding Rowena's cool hand. Her face is at peace and once again angelic. She has been relieved of her burden. But I have not. I don't know the words.

And from behind that old square wooden door, I hear the rustling of wool and the creaking of limbs.

HYDROPHOBIA

He plunged again into inky darkness, drowning in putrid liquid. It felt clammy and viscous against his skin. Down he sank, unable to scream. He thrashed his limbs and knew what would come next. Soon the gnarled fingers would grab him and pull him into that infernal embrace. Some fates are worse than death.

"There's Marine World," Cody said, one hand leaving the steering wheel to point at a weather-beaten blue and white building squatting in the center of a dusty gravel lot.

"You mean, there *was* Marine World," his girlfriend, Kristy corrected him with a hint of teasing in her voice.

"I've never heard of it," Kristy's younger brother Tim commented from the back seat of Cody's blue Sunbird.

"Your parents never took you?" Cody spun the wheel and turned into the weed-ridden lot. "It was pretty cool back when I was a kid. They had trained seals, dolphins, even penguins. Let's pull over and check it out. Maybe we can see in through a window."

Kristy frowned. "I heard the building was condemned or something."

"They just went out of business and cleared out in a hurry, that's all," Cody said.

"I mean after that."

Cody guided his car along the south side of the deserted structure. He looked at Kristy. "When?"

"God, Cody! Don't you remember the murders?"

"I doubt the killer is still lurking around in there."

The three of them clambered from the Sunbird and shuffled to the front entrance. The exterior paint was cracked and fading. Cody pressed his forehead against the glass door and shielded his eyes from the sun. He turned back to Kristy and her brother. "The glass is covered with tar paper or something from the inside. There's nothing to see."

"Oh, I bet there's a lot to see," Tim countered. "We just need to find a better place to look."

Kristy surveyed the weeds growing out of cracks in the asphalt. "How many years has this place been closed?"

"Only a couple," Cody replied. "I can't believe you never came here before."

"Dad wouldn't even take us to the mall." Tim said. "His idea of family time was watching TV together, and he picked all the shows."

"My favorite thing besides the dolphin show was the high diver..." Cody trailed off, his eyes gleaming. He began walking away from the front entrance and around the corner of the building.

"Where are you going?" Kristy asked.

"I want to see if the high dive platform is still back there."

Tim was already following Cody's lead. Shrugging, Kristy followed. The gate had been padlocked but some anonymous trailblazer had pried a couple boards loose from the fence a few yards farther down. The trio squeezed through the opening.

Discarded beer bottles and candy wrappers littered the ground. The empty bleachers gleamed in the burning summer sun. The high dive platform stood intact, although someone had removed the bottom rungs for safety's sake.

"Too bad," Cody remarked. "I wanted to show off my diving skills."

Kristy walked up beside him and gasped. The pool had never been drained. The water was dark green, almost black. "So that's what a swimming pool looks like if you shut the filtration system off for a couple years."

Tim picked up one of the empty bottles and lobbed it into the dark water. It landed with a dull splash and immediately sank. Kristy shivered against Cody as the bottle disappeared from view.

"That was creepy as hell," Tim said.

"Can you imagine someone accidentally falling in there with a bunch of drunks standing around?" Cody asked.

All three of them stood contemplating the pool and saying nothing.

"I think I'm ready to go," Kristy announced.

"I'm ready to explore inside," her brother countered.

"You could get in trouble for trespassing." Kristy's warning went unheeded; Tim was already prying the plywood from one of the back windows.

He yanked the covering off and leaned it against the building. "Too easy!" He stepped back to admire his work.

"How'd you manage that?" Cody asked him.

"It was already loose. Somebody probably went exploring in here before us."

Kristy shook her head. "I'm not crawling in there."

"We'll just go in for a minute or two," Cody promised. "Do you want to wait for us on the bleachers?"

"No thanks. That pool gives me the creeps. I'll be in the car."

"Honk if the cops show up," Tim joked.

"If they do, I'm ditching you guys."

Tim and Cody climbed in through the window into the empty cinder block shell that had once been Marine World.

After pausing momentarily to let their eyes adjust to the dim interior, Cody pointed. "I think this is where the seals were kept."

Along the back wall, next to the window they had just climbed through, were three small oval-shaped pools. Each appeared to be ten feet wide and about three feet deep and like the high dive pool, still full. Cody wrinkled his nose at the acrid smell permeating from the pools.

Tim barked laughter. One of the pools, they both saw, still contained a dirty red rubber ball. "How fast did these guys clear out, anyway?"

"I dunno." Cody led the way to where light was pouring in through several grimy windows. On the floor beside the last seal pool was an old manual credit card imprinter.

Tim kicked it and sent it skittering across the concrete. "What's in there?" Tim pointed at a pair of steel doors at the end of the corridor and to their right.

"That's the entrance to the aquarium area. If you keep walking, you've got the gift shop to the right, the main entrance directly in front of you and the pool where the dolphins performed on your left. The doors are probably locked though."

"Let's try anyway," Tim insisted. "I want to check it out. If they're unlocked, we can prop the doors open and just look in if it's too dark."

Tim tested the handle on one of the doors and it opened with a burst of stale air. The pair gazed into the darkness.

"I almost expected a horde of rats to come pouring out," Cody said.

Tim retrieved the manual credit card imprinter and wedged it under the door.

The pair shuffled inside a few steps then stopped to let their eyes adjust before they moved on. The aquarium area had been completely cleared out. Cody sneezed, wiped his hand on his pant leg and sneezed again. "It must be mold."

A few more steps deeper into the darkness, Tim spoke. "What would happen if the doors slammed shut behind us right about now?"

Cody chuckled nervously. It echoed loudly in the hollow expanse they were traversing. They gingerly made their way forward in the darkness. Once their shoes crunched over broken glass, but mostly the floor was free of obstructions.

"It looks a little brighter up ahead." Cody said. His voice betrayed a sense of relief he wouldn't admit to aloud.

A skylight in the ceiling proved to be the source of the light. A small square of sunlight fell in through the panes and seemed to lie listlessly on the floor, unmindful of the dust motes that danced in its warmth.

They stood near the sunbeam like nomads at an oasis. Ahead, they could see that someone had padlocked a chain around the front door handles. The windows were covered with tar paper. The admission counter, where years before bored teenagers sold tickets to sunburnt tourists, stood coated with dust but intact. The cash register and other retail business essentials were long gone.

Cody and Tim walked to the entrance of the gift shop. Peering in, they saw that the room was empty. Even the fixtures had been removed. Crossing through the little patch of sunlight, the pair approached the entrance to the dolphin show.

"Is this the only room left that we haven't explored?" Tim asked.

"Yeah," Cody replied. "Back when this place was open, this was where they had the trained dolphins jumping through hoops and leaping up to grab fish from people's hands."

Tim walked through the arched doorway at an angle. "I'm going to walk along the wall."

"You're going to walk right into the bleachers if you go that way. Walk this direction instead."

Cody heard Tim cursing and laughed as he visualized him stumbling against the first row of metal seats. "Hit your shins?"

His own feet hit a concrete obstruction and Cody threw his arms out reflexively.

Cody's mind screamed a warning to his body, but it was too late. He realized he'd stumbled on the concrete wall skirting the dolphin pool, but where Tim had the next few rows of bleachers to break his fall, he had nothing to stop his forward motion. Cody twisted and tried to throw his weight backwards but it was futile. His heart seemed to stop as he pitched headlong into the darkness. Before he could cry out his body splashed into the murky water. Cody had never been a strong swimmer and the concept of floating fled from his mind in an instant. He kicked and flailed in a blind panic. The water felt slimy and cold as it enveloped his limbs. The organic reek of the rotting algae was mixed with another odor. It was what he imagined the stench of rotting flesh would be; a taint of death that first filled his nostrils then invaded his mouth. Cody tried to cry out but choked on the viscous liquid instead.

The more he struggled, the further he sank. The combination of complete darkness and a seemingly bottomless pit of slime conspired to erase any rational thought. Cody somehow resisted the overwhelming urge to scream as the waters closed over his head.

Down he sank. His mind reeled. *This can't be happening! It shouldn't be this easy to die!*

Cody's knees and palms sank into muck as he settled to the bottom of the dolphin pool. He felt as if the weight of an ocean were crushing his lungs. He realized that now he at least knew which way was up. His feet slipped on the slimy surface of the pool floor. Cody reached up with both hands with the half-formed idea of attempting to lunge back to the surface.

Something cold and spongy leaned in and touched his palms. Repulsed, Cody shoved it away. He wondered if a dead dolphin were floating in the pool with him. Then he sensed the thing returning toward him, like a balloon tied to his wrist. His lungs were screaming now, and purple lights flashed behind his eyes. Cody crouched and then pushed toward the surface with what little reserve of strength he could muster.

Something caught his shirt and dragged him back down. Cody flailed out again. His hands brushed against something hard and slippery. *Bones? But just a moment ago it had felt like...*

The lights in his head were now gold and pulsing rapidly. Cody tried to get away but couldn't. He felt his clenched left hand being pried open. Something cold and hard slid onto his finger and the vise-like grip loosened. Cody felt the presence fading but then something brushed against his arms again. Too weak to swim now, he could only kneel and allow whatever was touching him to do as it wished.

Something small, soft and clammy wrapped around his right index finger. Cody experienced a horrifying moment of clarity; then he sank and knew no more.

Cody stroked and kicked through the water. He cried out in relief as he surged up and broke through the surface. A spray of water chilled him and he opened his eyes to the drab fluorescent interior of a small room. He was in a hospital bed, not the dolphin pool.

An overturned cup lay on a tray next to his bed. Its contents soaked the sheets and Cody shuddered. He concluded that he'd knocked the cup of water over while dreaming. At that moment, the door opened and a nurse entered. She was short and stout with eyes that hinted at good humor bubbling just below the surface.

"How did I get here?" he croaked as she approached his bedside.

"You came close to punching your ticket. We're concerned about your lungs because of all the algae in the water. My name's Lois, by the way." She checked the IV bag hanging at the head of the bed. "We've got you on antibiotics to fight infection, and you probably don't feel too hot right now, but we do expect you to make a full recovery."

Cody closed his eyes and sank back onto his pillow. His lungs ached and his eyes itched with maddening intensity. *I'll be okay. I'll never go near a pool again and I'll never toss a coin in a fountain and Sea World will never be on my vacation list and that mop bucket out in the hall makes me want to scream but I'll be okay.* Cody trembled.

"Thank the good Lord that your brother-in-law is such a good swimmer," Lois continued. "I understand he's the one who saved you."

"So Tim jumped in and found me in time..." Cody mulled it over. As an afterthought he added, "He's my girlfriend's brother, though, not my brother-in-law."

Lois raised her eyebrows. "Well the way that little brunette was crying, I assumed you two were already paired up." Cody felt a pleasant blush blooming on his cheeks.

"I guess that fooled me too." Lois pointed toward his left hand. Cody looked down and gasped. A tarnished gold band circled his ring finger.

Cody's vision began to narrow into a tunnel. His head spun and he relived the sensation of skeletal fingers sliding the ring onto his finger. *'With this ring, I thee wed.'*

Cody began to choke, feeling water that wasn't really there crawl down his windpipe again. He heard Lois calling his name, but she seemed very far away. Another voice drowned hers out.

'Don't go yet; there's someone I want you to meet...' The fingers that wrapped around his were tiny, cold and insistent. He wasn't sure if the howl he heard came from his lips or the baby's.

Cody lunged forward in his bed, accidentally tearing the IV from his arm and knocking Lois back. The sound of the commotion drew a pair of orderlies and a doctor who quickly administered a shot to calm him.

Even in a sedative-induced haze, Cody realized that his 'new family' had found him on the cusp of death. He felt sorrow on behalf of the two lonely souls in the dolphin pool. He thought maybe their grief and confusion kept their spirits trapped there. Cody tried to picture the monster that could do such a thing to his family.

Cody would tell the police about the bodies. Maybe their discovery and proper burial would give them peace.

But what if it wasn't enough? What if he was now inextricably linked to the tragic pair? Would he forever be haunted by their memory? Or would he be haunted by something both more *and* less substantial?

All Cody knew for sure was that every time he floated into sleep, the cold, wet, rotting forms of the dead woman and her baby rose up from the darkness to greet him.

A STORY ABOUT MONSTERS

The bad thing was going to happen again. Even though I'd wished on a falling star that it wouldn't, the bad thing was going to happen. Again.

I could hear Stepdaddy Ray out in the hall. Then my bedroom door opened and he was a black shadow with light behind him, like a reverse-angel. He closed the door behind him and my room got filled with dark. I heard the dull thump of his whiskey bottle when he set it on my dresser, then the floorboards creaked as he came toward me.

I lay still.

I pretended I was asleep and dreaming.

I was in a coma.

I was *dead*.

I could hear Stepdaddy Ray breathing now, almost panting. The starlight that snuck through my window was enough for me to see that his hands were moving. One of them was, anyway.

Then Stepdaddy Ray froze. He looked at his feet.

Something yanked Stepdaddy Ray to the floor. His head cracked real loud on the wood. I sat up to watch. His face was a white blur as he slid under my bed. It happened so fast I almost thought I only imagined it. When the crunching of bones and wet sucking sounds came, I decided I hadn't imagined it after all.

I stared at the ceiling and wrapped my pillow around my ears. I woulda gotten slapped for being that loud at the dinner table.

I was so focused on trying to ignore what was going on underneath me that I didn't hear my mama coming. She threw open my bedroom door and stood there with her hands on her hips.

"She givin' you trouble, Ray?" Mama's voice was shrill. She flipped on the overhead light and squinted at me. "I heard a noise."

"He was gonna hurt me again." I tried to explain. I wished Mama would run up and hold me, but she just looked mad.

"What'd you do to Ray?"

"Nothin', Mama, I swear!"

"Where is he then?" Mama stopped and stared at the floor beside my bed. The look on her face made me think maybe a skunk had got in somehow. I peeped over the edge of the mattress. There was dark red stuff splattered on the floor.

"You uppity little bitch! You should be thankful for the attention!" She spun around and went to my dresser. I don't know why, but the way my mama was acting reminded me of the day I heard my teacher, Mrs. Amos, telling another lady that my mama was not right in the head. I didn't try to argue with Mrs. Amos because I figured she was right.

"I'm gonna punish you dearly for hurtin' him," Mama growled. She grabbed the half empty whiskey bottle and threw it at me. I ducked and the bottle shattered against the wall, spraying everything. What a mess!

My bed sheets smelled stinky, like Stepdaddy Ray's breath when he's up close and on me, and I wrinkled my nose. I started to crawl out of bed, going real slow and careful because of the pieces of broken glass. I didn't want to get all cut up. Mama fished around in her bathrobe and before I got very far I saw her hold up her lighter. All of a sudden, I got real scared.

"Oh, Mama, no! Please, please, please NO!" I tried not to sound like a whiny baby but it was really hard. Mama's eyes had a funny look in them; like she was happy and mad and scared and sad all at the same time. I couldn't look away from those eyes so I just sat there like I was froze.

My closet door flew open so hard it busted right off the hinges and something dark hurtled out from inside. It landed on Mama's back and they both crashed to the floor. The thing looked like a big ball of dirty, matted black fur, like a *monster*. I thought the top half of its body was going to tip over backwards from the rest of it, but then I saw that the monster was just opening its mouth. I looked away and counted glass shards in my covers for a while. When I looked up again, it was too soon. I seen the monster sitting on my floor, munching away. Sticking out of its mouth was Mama's hand, still holding her lighter.

Then the light started to fade and everything got real dark real fast. All I saw was black and I don't remember what happened next.

I was eating dry cereal in the kitchen when the police man knocked on the door the next morning. He said somebody and called to complain about some noises from last night.

I told him that my mama had been hollering at me and was fixing to start me on fire but that she hadn't. I also said that she wasn't in the house anymore. I guess I didn't lie.

The police man didn't look very happy and he asked me to show him where it happened. We went upstairs to my bedroom and there was the lighter on the floor and the broken glass on the bed. The police man smelled my bed sheets and looked even less happy. He hustled me out of the room but one thing I noticed before he got me out of there was that the blood on my floor was all gone. The monster under my bed liked Stepdaddy Ray enough to lick the plate, I guess. I could tell just by how the house felt that all the monsters were gone.

Some people came to take me away.

Nobody saw Mama or Stepdaddy Ray ever again. They sure looked for them, though.

Finally, I got sent to live in a new house with a new family. It is very nice here. I get to eat lots of good food and they have a puppy that is really funny and always wants to play. Plus, my new mama and dad never yell at me or try to start me on fire or hurt me down there. My new mama is named Carole, but I call her Mama Foster because I heard people call her my Foster Mother. My new daddy is named Neal. He tells me bedtime stories. Sometimes he tells me silly stories about monsters hiding under my bed or in my closet and I just laugh.

There aren't any monsters living in my room now. I think good monsters only visit kids who need protecting. In this house, the good monsters aren't needed, because there aren't any *bad* monsters sleeping right down the hall.

THE ARTIST AND HIS SUBJECT

The woman in front of me must be feeding a family of ten, Cassie thought. She shifted her grocery basket from one hand to the other and stretched her free fingers, letting them relax.

As the beleaguered cashier slowly scanned the items, space opened little by little for Cassie's modest selections. She tucked a loose lock of blond hair behind her ear and carefully lined up two tins of Vienna sausage, eight packages of Ramen noodles—you had to buy eight to get the sale price—and a half gallon of skim milk. The milk wasn't the generic brand; Cassie had let herself splurge on 'the good milk.' The woman finished paying and pushed her heavily laden cart toward the exit. For no real reason, Cassie thought of an old west trapper, coaxing and prodding a pack mule along a desolate mountain pass. She giggled.

"That comes to five seventy eight," the cashier announced. Cassie handed the woman four ones, and four quarters.

"There's the five," Cassie said, flashing her best smile. The cashier offered no visible response. Cassie dug in her pocket. As she retrieved her remaining change and began counting it out on her palm she silently prayed that she had enough. The milk had been thirty cents higher this week and Cassie secretly felt terrified at the prospect of coming up short.

That had only happened once, almost two months ago. She'd been daydreaming as she shopped and was startled to hear the total. Upon realizing that she was a full dollar and thirteen cents short, she stammered that she'd have to put something back. This announcement had been met by tight-lipped indifference from the cashier and a smirk from the teen standing in line behind her.

Isn't this delightful, Cassie had thought bitterly. She began to ask the cashier if she could put back the head of lettuce when a sympathetic voice spoke up.

"Don't put anything back, dear. I've got a few dollars to help you along," an elderly woman a few places back said, in a voice loud enough for several lanes of shoppers to hear.

Cassie felt her cheeks flush.

"That's really not necessary," she began.

"Just take it," the kid interrupted. Cassie realized he was ogling the outline of her breasts. "Just cuz you're kinda hot don't mean I wanna stand behind you *all day*."

Cassie's slight flush blossomed into a deep blush. She never shopped without keeping a running total in her mind ever since.

Still, she felt her heart beating faster as she counted the dirty change out on her sweating palm. She needn't have worried. Cassie ended up with fifty-two cents to spare.

"And seventy eight," Cassie said, handing over the money. The cashier wordlessly gave her the receipt.

"Thank you." Cassie said then added tentatively, "I hope you have a nice day."

The woman looked surprised and stared at Cassie with watery blue eyes, as if noticing her for the first time.

"I hope you have a nice day too." she said, sounding sincere.

Cassie smiled and turned to go.

The cashier had begun scanning the next customer's items, but she raised her voice over the scanner's electronic chirp. "Let's meet here again tomorrow and we'll compare notes." Cassie and the cashier laughed and Cassie strolled away.

As she passed through the first set of automatic doors, she glanced at the bulletin board. Once she had noticed a want ad from someone asking for help with housekeeping. It turned out to only be temporary—the woman had suffered a broken wrist—but it was a great opportunity for Cassie to pick up some extra cash. Ever since then, her eyes automatically went to the board.

Today, somebody had lost their pet cat and was offering a reward for its return, while another person was giving away kittens 'free to good homes.' Cassie thought it ironic and somehow sad. She smiled when she saw the business card of a real estate agent with the unfortunate name, Guy Mann. Then she saw an ad on plain white paper, with plain black type. It read:

Artistic Subject Wanted
Will pay
Please call

The simple message concluded with a phone number.

Cassie plucked the stick pin from the board and deftly caught the floating piece of paper with her other hand. Then she fished in her pocket for her last two remaining quarters and stepped to the pay phone. This sounded interesting. *And maybe I won't have to eat Ramen noodles every night next week*, Cassie thought. The phone rang twice in her ear and then:

"Hello?" A man's voice, quiet and calm.

"Hi, I'm calling about the ad for an artistic subject..." Cassie trailed off, not sure what to say next.

"Of course." The man's voice was very soft. Cassie found it oddly comforting. "Are you interested in the position? I have an immediate need."

"Well, I'm certainly interested in knowing what it is that you do." Cassie replied. "But I'm not sure if the job is something I'd be interested in just yet."

"I would be happy to show you first," the man replied agreeably. "We could interview each other, so to speak. Might you be able to stop by right away?"

"I think so. I mean, sure," Cassie amended.

"You'll want to bring along the ad itself," the man said.

Cassie was puzzled. "Why?"

"Turn it over."

Cassie did. Directions from the grocery store to the artist's home were printed on the back.

* * *

The large house Cassie arrived in front of was a mansion by anyone's standards. She parked her car on the side of a large circular brick driveway. Lush hedges hid most of the house from the street. Cassie felt a twinge of jealousy at the home's beauty and seclusion. She rang the doorbell and unconsciously held her breath.

Please let me get this job, she prayed, *but please don't let his idea of an 'artistic subject' be a girl who'll pose naked while he gets off.*

The door swung open and Cassie came face to face with a well dressed little man who smiled at her, bowed cordially and then beckoned her inside. Charmed, Cassie entered and surveyed the interior.

The sitting room was tastefully furnished with rich mahogany furniture. Gorgeous paintings of nature scenes decorated the walls. A polished coffee table squatted near the center of the room in front of a large black leather couch. Hundreds of books filled an enormous bookcase. Cassie marveled.

"Won't you sit down?" The man gestured toward the couch and Cassie perched on the edge. "Can I offer you a glass of ice water?"

"Yes, thank you." Cassie replied automatically. The artist poured her a glass from a crystal pitcher sweating onto a silver tray placed in the middle of the table. Cassie sipped her water and glanced at an elaborate art tableau situated on the far side of the room.

"You live here in the city?" the man asked.

"Yes."

"From here originally?"

"No. I'm from upstate. I was going to school at the community college, but needed to take a semester off."

"You are saving up for tuition to continue. Am I right?"

"Yes," Cassie admitted and sipped her ice water. She hoped it would cool the embarrassed flush from her cheeks.

"And are you working currently?"

"The job market has been less than ideal."

The man threw back his head and laughed. If Cassie felt rattled by the man's line of questioning, he put her at ease again with that reaction.

"Perhaps I can help you," he remarked.

Cassie nodded took another sip and glanced again at the art piece against the far wall.

"Would you like to take a closer look?" the artist invited. "That is one of my favorite pieces."

Cassie stood, swaying briefly. She felt a little lightheaded from standing up too quickly but carefully crossed the room.

It was a sculpture, Cassie saw, composed of seven ivory colored forearms reaching upward. Above, a small spotlight was mounted on the ceiling, casting a heavenly glow down on the cluster of reaching arms. A lush red velvet tapestry covered the base of the display. Cassie noted that the 'fingernails' were painted a shade that matched the velvet base. The effect was striking and, in Cassie's opinion, completely original.

"I call that piece 'Supplication'," the man said from behind her.

From the sound of his voice, Cassie knew he was still on the far side of the room, yet his words swirled around her shoulders and into her ears like smoke.

"To me it conveys the relationship between mankind and a higher power," the artist continued. "Or, you may find it symbolic of victims and their oppressor."

His voice had taken on a rather egotistic tone that Cassie didn't much care for. She was mesmerized by the piece however.

"So you take plaster casts?" Cassie heard herself asking. "Or do you do all the sculpting by hand?"

She felt another wave of dizziness wash over her. The hands blurred, as if waving goodbye. Despite drinking the better part of a glass of ice water, all the saliva had dried up in her mouth.

When the man didn't answer Cassie turned around to look at him. He stood at his front door. Both her host and the living room appeared fuzzy and drifted in and out of focus.

"My dear, I am not a sculptor at all," the artist replied as he padlocked the door that lead back to the safety of the outside world. "I am a taxidermist."

* * *

Cassie smelled a pungent chemical odor. She felt like a cork bobbing in water, but realized that though her body seemed to be in motion she could not move her arms or legs. Cassie heard soft footfalls, a rhythmic squeaking and someone's rapid shallow breathing. She realized the breathing was her own. Her mouth felt like it was filled with sand. Cassie tried to open her eyes but the lids seemed glued shut.

Her forward momentum suddenly ceased and Cassie's head drooped forward so that she could feel her chin on her chest.

"We shall begin our tour here," a male voice quietly announced. Cassie's brain reeled in confusion for several moments then the events of the afternoon snapped into focus.

Get up and run away from him! Cassie mentally commanded. She might have told herself to burst into flames or sprout wings and fly with more success. Surrounded by darkness and unable to move her limbs, Cassie could only wait. The hands of her captor caressed her shoulders and she shuddered.

"Allow me to show you what no other living person has ever seen," the little man invited. Cassie felt his fingers slide up her cheeks and she cringed.

Light flooded in, drowning all other sensory information as she squinted at the sudden change. The self-proclaimed artist had removed her blindfold. He'd apparently brought her to the end of a long hallway. To Cassie's left a beige wall retreated away from them. To her right she saw what looked like a series of cells, as in a prison, but without the bars. She glanced down and saw that her captor had removed all of her clothing and had used leather straps to tie her arms, legs and torso to a chrome wheelchair.

The initial shock from the brightness began to wear off and the man's carefully enunciated words gradually rose to the surface of her consciousness. "As you will soon see, my museum is a work in progress."

Cassie looked again at the 'holding cells' and realized they were actually a series of small shallow rooms designed to house her captor's artistic creations. *What was the last thing he had said?* Cassie struggled to remember.

His words came back to her like a cup of scalding coffee tossed in her face. *'I am a taxidermist.'*

She considered him to be a kidnapper, murderer and madman. But her captor obviously thought of himself as an artist above all else. Cassie shuddered again as she realized that he was about to force her on a guided tour of his 'artistic' creations.

"I adore literature," the man was saying. "And I try to convey my appreciation with my art. Each tableau is a representation of a key moment from one of my favorite novels. This first one for instance—" Her captor abruptly wheeled her chair forward and two figures seemed to lurch into view. Cassie gasped. Beside her, the artist beamed.

"Your reaction is exactly how I felt when I read the passage where Lennie accidentally kills Curley's wife!" Cassie gaped at the green glassy eyes of the slumping woman. Her gaze traveled up to the face of the hulking behemoth that held the dead woman. His bright blue glass eyes were set imperfectly in their sockets.

"That's by design," the artist quickly revealed when he'd followed her gaze. "The man I used as my subject was the right size physically but had no mental defects. I had to compensate by adjusting the eyes to convey Lennie's shortcomings."

Cassie remained silent. To her, the unnatural poses and contorted faces of the man and woman were a mockery of humanity.

"Have you read Steinbeck's *Of Mice and Men*?" her captor asked. Cassie shook her head. His lips pressed into a thin white line and he stepped back behind her chair. "This next display was actually my first creation."

Cassie's eyes swam with tears. A little boy of perhaps ten reached out with one arm into the pocket of the other figure, a man in a black cloak and top hat. The boy's face and hands were dirty and his clothes were shabby and threadbare. "The irony here is rather humorous and worth mentioning," the artist prattled. "The wealthy 'mark' was actually a homeless transient, while my street urchin was obtained on his way home from a prestigious private school." He grinned at Cassie as if waiting for her to share his enthusiasm. Instead she felt nausea threaten to overwhelm her. *Obtained?* Cassie didn't want to look at the abomination on display so she gazed at her captor instead.

"Surely you must recognize this one," he said and raised his eyebrows. "The boy is the Artful Dodger from *Oliver Twist* by Dickens. Doesn't that ring a bell?"

Cassie shook her head and the little man made a show of groaning aloud. Then he sighed and pushed her forward to the next exhibit. Cassie wrinkled her nose in surprised disgust. Two large hogs stood on hind legs on either side of a small table covered with playing cards and shot glasses. The swine's lips were curled into malicious smirks that made them look surprisingly human. "And here are Karl and Dick," the artist announced.

"At least they're not humans," Cassie whispered. It was the first time she had spoken since regaining consciousness.

The little man only scowled. "That was a joke. They're obviously Napoleon and Snowball from George Orwell's *Animal Farm*."

"I don't know what you're talking about and I want to go home now," Cassie told him.

He gaped at her, mouth hanging open. "For God's sake! It's an easy read!" Spittle flew from his mouth and Cassie felt convinced that he would lash out and strike her. Instead he angrily shoved her wheelchair forward.

Cassie saw that a wall of stone and mortar hid the next exhibit from view. "I hand-sewed the jester's costume for this artistic subject myself, then hid my handiwork behind this wall that I built, stone by stone. But I suppose the ingenuity of my homage to Poe's *The Cask of Amontillado* is lost on a blonde zero like you."

The artist scowled and they moved forward again. The next scene rolled into view and Cassie cried out. She clenched her hands into fists of impotent fury. A hairy, naked man sneered in glassy-eyed lust from his position on top of a grimacing teenage girl. The bed sheets lay crumpled at the foot of the bed. "I needed help getting this one just right," the madman admitted. "Nabokov's *Lolita* had a profound effect on me. To lend this scene authenticity, I let my 'Humbert' get into character first before I took his life—"

"You're fucking insane!" Cassie shrieked. Hot tears scalded her cheeks. Fueled by vindictive rage she struggled against the straps that held her down. "This is not art! This is garbage excreted by a diseased and depraved mind!"

The little man staggered back as if she'd struck him. All the color drained from his face. Cassie hoped her captor would sprawl onto the concrete in a dead faint. But any glimmer of hope she had was immediately snuffed out as the little man instead leaned forward until their noses were almost touching. His skin was ashen but his eyes glittered with the juices of insanity and cold fury.

"You ignorant pinhead! How DARE you criticize my art!" He straightened abruptly, chin up and chest out. "I thought you might appreciate what I have painstakingly created, but I see now that I was gravely mistaken."

He moved her chair forward for the last time. The next display was incomplete. A man in his late twenties or early thirties posed awkwardly in one corner. Cassie would have found him handsome if he were still alive.

Her eyes skimmed over an array of liquid-filled jugs, scalpel blades, heavy duty scissors, knives and other objects she could not readily identify, neatly arranged on a large rolling tray table. She immediately understood their sinister purpose.

Another rolling tray table held an odd assortment of items and Cassie scowled in confusion at the bottle of olive oil, the Brie, and a pile of nails beside a hammer.

"That's a prop cart," the artist explained, but Cassie felt more confused and unsettled than ever.

The artist lifted the footrests of the wheel chair into the air and locked them into place. Did he intend to break her legs? Cassie struggled vainly and watched as he strode across the tiny room. He retrieved a large plastic tube from the table. He held it behind his back so she couldn't see what it contained.

"This is my most ambitious project. I will painstakingly recreate the most shocking scene in the novel. I'll film the process for reference. That way I'll be able to preserve you and your attacker in the most realistic pose possible."

A sheen of sweat glistened on the artist's forehead. He grinned like a rabid hyena.

"Your facial expression, how much exposed organ tissue is created as a result, how your body will contort; I won't have anything less than perfection in my masterpiece."

The artist stepped forward and stood between Cassie's outstretched naked legs. His sweaty hands struggled to twist the lid from the plastic tube.

The artist expected Cassie to start screaming but she disappointed him one final time. She only stared blankly at the rat in the tube.

She hadn't read Bret Easton Ellis' *American Psycho* either.

THERE'S NO WORD FOR IT

There's no word to describe the fear I suffer from. I've looked, believe me. I found lots of other phobias, but not one that describes my situation. There's pnigophobia, which is the fear of choking or being smothered. Seems like a valid concern. Phagophobia is almost the opposite; it's the fear of swallowing. Then there's the marvelous trio of acarophobia, entomophobia and insectophobia. Those are all the fear of insects. Despite my current predicament, none of these phobias have wound their icy, irrational fears around my psyche the way *this* has. Yet I still haven't found the official word for my most prominent fear.

#

The first insect I accidentally swallowed was most likely a mosquito. I was playing with my four-year-old nephew, Caleb, when it happened. I chased him on all fours as he squealed and scampered across our front lawn. I opened my mouth for what I hoped was a passable imitation of an angry bark and saw a small dot of black with cellophane wings darting through the air. The mosquito collided with the back of my throat and I swallowed automatically. I felt the prickle on the back of my throat where the mosquito had landed, but after a drink of cool water from the kitchen tap, the feeling went away. I thought no more about the incident until the second insect flew into my mouth later that same day.

It was after dinner, our visitors had gone, and I was puttering around outside. I started to yawn and caught a glimpse of green. Before I could react, I felt a tickle at the back of my throat.

I'd decided that it had been a green midge due to its coloring when I heard the low motor-like buzz of a bumblebee. It was joined by the electric drone of a horsefly. High pitched squealing in both ears announced the arrival of at least two more mosquitoes. I walked at first, and then jogged toward my front door, flailing my arms in an attempt at staving off the sudden swarm of insects. I unleashed a steam of expletives—and swallowed two bugs more before I made it inside.

#

That evening after the first wave of insects invaded my body, I almost took syrup of ipecac. Then I realized I'd rather let my stomach acid do its job than subject myself to the vomit-inducing wrath of that awful liquid. After all, I'd swallowed bugs, not poison. Looking back, I wish I had at least tried the ipecac, though I doubt it would have done any good.

Instead I did what any sane person would do; I tried to rationalize the situation. Failing at this, I fell back on the next best solution. I pretended that nothing out of the ordinary had happened.

That night I dreamed that a cell phone kept vibrating in my stomach.

#

I felt fine upon waking the next morning. I brushed my teeth, showered and dressed for work without remembering the bugs. I grabbed my briefcase, shoved the door open and trotted down the steps toward the driveway. What I saw stopped me in my tracks. Mayflies carpeted the hood and roof of my Impala. Suddenly uneasy, I turned on my heel and hurried back up the stairs.

Once safely within the confines of my home I pulled the curtain aside and gazed out the living room's picture window. Still in her pajamas, my wife, Samantha, padded into the room.

"I thought you'd left."

"Come look at this."

Samantha leaned to look where I pointed. "What?"

"Don't you see the mayflies all over my car?"

"What are you talking about, Will? I don't see anything."

I squinted. The white Impala looked gold thanks to the multitude of mayflies perched on it, their iridescent wings reflecting in the sun. I coughed without really needing to, stalling for time. "I think I might need to take some time off," I finally muttered.

Samantha's eyes twinkled. "Of course I see the mayflies! I'm just messing with you!"

I love my wife dearly but sometimes she seems to get a little too much enjoyment from making me feel foolish. Still, Samantha's beauty makes it easy for me to forgive her.

"Would you do me a huge favor?" I asked. "Would you go out there with a newspaper or something and chase them away for me?"

She put her hands on her hips and arched one eyebrow skeptically.

"Humor me, just this once," I begged.

Moments later, I watched from the window as Samantha approach my car holding yesterday's paper. She swung the makeshift weapon onto the hood and the mayflies took off *en masse,* creating a golden cloud that dissipated into the morning sky.

My wife grinned at me triumphantly. I hurried out to her. "I squashed a few and the rest flew off."

"Thanks honey." I kissed the top of her head. "This may sound crazy, but I was almost convinced that those things were deliberately waiting for me."

We laughed, and in that brief moment, a mayfly that had concealed itself beneath a crease in my wife's pajamas took to the air and flew into my mouth. The flutter of wings as it journeyed down my throat elicited a coughing fit within me. I pulled away from Samantha as the coughs wracked my frame. Then the feeling was gone, the newcomer apparently having joined its comrades.

During my commute, the wings of the crushed mayflies waved at me gaily from the hood of my Impala, proud martyrs in the war against my sanity.

#

Insects targeted me for the next three days. They flew—and sometimes crawled—into my mouth at every opportunity. I saw a few miller moths, although they easily could have been meal moths. A honey bee hovered around my head for several minutes before giving up. A bumblebee tried to fly into my mouth but I slapped it aside at the last second. It stung the back of my hand instead. I damn near choked to death when that gladiator katydid crawled down my throat.

I broke down and tried the syrup of ipecac. It made me vomit, but to my great dismay no dead insects appeared in the toilet bowl.

Thursday afternoon, on my way home from work, I stopped at Bloom Hardware and scooped up an armload of insect repellents. I waddled up and down the aisles, cradling my brood of aerosol cans, spray bottles and baited traps. As an afterthought, I selected a package of those white filter masks you sometimes see allergy-prone people wear when they're out mowing.

"Bug problems?" the cashier asked as I unloaded my selections down on the counter.

I started to reply and right at that moment a ladybug sped through the air and straight down my gullet. I felt tears of frustration well up, and I glowered at the clerk.

"What the hell is a ladybug doing in a hardware store anyway? Don't you people spray against that kind of thing?"

#

Samantha smiled at the array of insect repellents I had purchased. She waited patiently as I grimly squirted the windowsills and around our doors, both inside and out. When my hand ached from pumping the spray handle, I simply switched to the other hand. I sprayed our hedges, the exteriors of our vehicles, the mailbox, and everything else I could think of. I even dragged the wooden ladder from the garage and sprayed around all the exteriors of the windows on the second floor. I positioned poisoned bait traps in every corner and hung flypaper from the ceiling of each room. After three hours I staggered into the bedroom. I felt dizzy from the effects of the chemicals and there was a buzzing in my ears.

Samantha, now in her pajamas, wordlessly laid out a bath towel and turned on the shower for me. She wasn't smiling any more.

I cleaned up, toweled off and pulled on my pajamas. I couldn't get the insects out of my mind. Haunted by a vision of a caravan of bugs marching across my pillow and into my mouth while I slept, I returned to the hardware store bag on the kitchen counter. I pulled on one of the white filter masks and fitted it over my mouth and nose. Samantha looked alarmed as I crawled under the covers beside her.

"Will," she entreated. "I love you, but don't you think you're taking this a little too far?"

"Something is making insects want to fly in through my mouth to my stomach," I declared. "That's not natural, damn it! Until I find out what's going on, the mask stays on."

"Look, I'm sorry this is happening to you."

"I'll check in the phone book tomorrow morning," I assured her as I clicked off the lamp. "A specialist will know what to do."

Samantha rolled toward me and pecked my cheek above the white mask.

"Good night, sleep tight, don't let the bed bugs bite," she said and giggled uncertainly. Then she rolled away from me. I didn't try to comfort or reassure her. I'd become preoccupied with the buzzing again. I could still hear it, but it wasn't in my ears like I had first thought. The buzzing came from my stomach.

#

The next morning, I sat on the edge of the bathtub and evacuated my bowels. It took longer than I'd expected to overcome the urge to sit on the toilet. At last I was able to break from of my deeply ingrained directive. After wiping, I pulled on a pair of Samantha's dishwashing gloves and began to systematically and carefully examine my feces.

"What are you doing, Will?"

I jumped at the sound of my wife's voice. "I am conducting an examination of my excrement." Part of me realized how ridiculous I must have sounded. You can't polish a turd, after all. "I'm doing this in hopes of finding wings, legs or some other evidence that the insects are dying and being naturally expelled."

Still kneeling, my arms hanging limply over the edge of the tub, I stole a glance over my shoulder. Samantha's face had paled. She didn't say a word. Instead, she took a careful step back, turned on her heel and hurried down the hallway. I heard the front door open and close. I held my breath until I heard the distant sound of her car starting. I listened as she drove away. I wondered when she'd be back.

Even more troubling, I found no insect presence in my feces.

#

Although I went to work on Friday, I accomplished little in my preoccupied state. I asked my supervisor for the next week off, citing health issues. I then spent the weekend dousing the house with more insect repellent. Each morning I examined my bowel movements but was disappointed by the results.

Samantha phoned me Sunday evening to say that although she was worried about me she would be staying with friends until I had resolved my issues. That's what she called them; *issues*, not problems. I assured her that I had made seeing a doctor my top priority.

When Monday arrived, the first ear, nose and throat specialist I contacted refused to take me seriously. It was the same with the second one I called, and with the third. The general practitioner at Bloom Memorial Hospital who fit me in on short notice refused to examine me once he had heard my complaint. Instead he gave me the business card of a psychologist who practiced nearby. Out of spite, I slipped a stethoscope into my jacket after the jackass had left the room and shredded the business card on my way out.

At home, I sat in my leather recliner and used the purloined instrument to listen to the cacophony of buzzing, chirping and droning coming from inside my distended stomach.

If doctors weren't going to hear me out long enough to actually help me, I'd have to find another way. I'd have to arrange for an 'accidental' discovery of the insects within me. I ruminated on the matter while attempting to drown my unwelcome guests in scotch.

After a couple of hours and double that many scotches I felt I had concocted a foolproof idea: gastric bypass surgery. During the procedure the doctor would surely see that something was amiss.

I lay back in my recliner, feeling very self-satisfied. Even though I had tossed the stethoscope aside, I could still hear the bugs. In fact, it was the interior chirping of crickets that eventually lulled me to sleep.

#

"I'm sorry sir, but based on the information you have provided, you simply are not a candidate for gastric bypass surgery." The woman from Bloom Memorial sounded bored.

"You don't understand." I clutched the receiver in one hand and rubbed my churning stomach with the other. "I *need* this!"

"I'm sorry. You simply don't weigh enough to—"

"Damn it, listen to me! I need someone to take a look at my stomach!"

"Sir, if you'll calm down, I will explain your options to you." Now the woman sounded both bored and annoyed simultaneously.

"I'm calm," I lied.

"I would advise you to call your health insurance company. You have to understand that this would fall into the category of elective surgery. Most likely your insurance company will not cover the procedure, but you should contact them first for possible pre-approval. They might let you apply the cost of the procedure toward your deductible," the woman prattled.

My hands shook. I felt sick. The scotch was long gone and I'd moved on to whiskey. Since Samantha was not in the house, I didn't bother using a glass. I swallowed my mounting panic and washed it down with a swig from the bottle. I fidgeted in my chair as the woman went on.

"Of course, whether or not we happen to be in-network providers with your particular insurance company will affect how much help you'd be getting from them. Depending on the plan you have, some insurance companies might require you to undergo a complete physical before allowing you to schedule elective surgery. Then there's the possibility that—"

Finally giving voice to my mounting revulsion, I shrieked and threw the phone across the room. An emergency room visit had taken two years of phone calls to my insurance company before it got paid. Always there were the loopholes, the missing paperwork, the additional information required. I couldn't face all that again.

Bugs were hell-bent on climbing into my mouth. I didn't need my insurance company trying to climb up my ass. Having a choice between 'A' and 'B' was no choice at all. There had to be an easier way.

I drained the contents of the bottle and mentally formulated my plan for deliverance. Having resolved myself on this alternate plan of action, I rose and headed for the kitchen. A lone fly pattering against the window pane turned its attention toward me as I entered. I grabbed my car keys off the counter and opened my mouth for the approaching fly. Why not one more for the road?

I careened toward Bloom Hardware, madly singing *"I Know an Old Lady Who Swallowed a Fly"*. I was halfway through my seventh rendition, gleefully bellowing "perhaps she'll diiiiiieeeee!" when I spun the wheel and guided the Impala into a handicapped spot near the store's entrance.

I left the car door hanging open and trotted into the store's interior. My stomach felt bloated, itchy, and unsettled. I was painfully conscious of every move the bugs were making inside me and I muttered under my breath, entreating them to keep still. It had begun to feel like an interior rash. I scanned the signs hanging above the aisles until I located the one I wanted: Gardening.

"Can I help you find anything today, sir?" asked the green-vested teenager who'd materialized beside me.

"I would like to obtain the strongest insecticide you have on hand. Not the stuff meant for household purposes, but something a farmer or a professional greenhouse would use."

"Sure. We keep that in the back."

"Would you please go get it and meet me back here as soon as you can?"

He nodded and we parted ways. The kid made it back in four minutes, but I was back in two. His eyebrows furrowed when he saw what I had acquired.

"Is that the strongest stuff you've got?" I lifted my chin toward the large black aerosol can he carried.

"Yes sir. Guaranteed to kill all types of insects on contact."

"I want you to pop the lid off that can and get ready to spray it. Understand?"

The kid had paled. His eyes seemed to be glued to the garden shears I held. "I should call my manager."

"Aim right here," I pointed at my midriff. "Get ready to spray..."

Envisioning a dishonored Samurai warrior, I lifted the shears over my head, and then swung down as hard as I could. There was a wet snap as the blades punctured the lining of my stomach. Before the pain kicked in full force, I pulled the wet blades back out, turned them at an angle in my right hand and sliced my stomach wide open.

"Now!" I bellowed.

Instead of insecticide, the kid sprayed his half-digested lunch out onto the tiled floor.

For my part, I sprayed profuse amounts of dark red blood, stomach bile and enough harbored insects to impress even Noah.

I became dimly aware of the kid shouting. I think he was trying to yell for an ambulance, but his words came out all garbled. Maybe I should have let him get his manager after all.

I glanced up at the army of insects that crawled, skittered, and hovered in the aisle around and above me. It was as if the multitude were considering the situation. I struggled toward the insecticide sprayer lying in the aisle where the kid had dropped it. I brandished the spray and the insects dissipated in all directions. They *finally* realized they were not welcome.

The sharp pain in my stomach was already fading, and a warm, muzzy feeling began to envelop me. I sank completely to the sticky tile, my head swimming. Darkness rapidly narrowed my field of vision.

I felt like laughing. I had won. I was free. Best of all, I didn't have to deal with my insurance company. The endless cycle of letters and phone calls; the rules, regulations, exclusions and the dreaded rejected claims.

What would one call a pronounced fear of, and aversion to, dealing with insurance companies? From what I have researched, there's no word for it.

BOOTLEGS FROM BOSTON

Clint Porter felt like he could cheerfully kill the woman standing across from him. The offensive odor of patchouli wafted from her so strongly that Clint wheezed and waddled on to the next vendor's booth. The music memorabilia flea market had always been a favorite weekend destination but today he felt sweaty, short of breath and irritable. Cash burned a hole in his pocket but he found nothing worth a second glance.

Most of the vendors stocked the same old vinyl; a few rare 45s, imports and a seemingly endless supply of routine crap that people could pick up at any rummage sale. Some of the tables showcased bootlegs on compact disc. He recognized the same shows he'd purchased years ago masquerading behind new covers. Clint turned up his nose in exaggerated disgust.

The booth at the end of the parking lot caught his eye and Clint lumbered forward for a closer look. The surface of the table was empty. Behind the table a wild-looking man perched in a canvas director's chair. Clint decided he looked like a half-crazy, elderly Frank Zappa.

"Afternoon. Help you find anything special?" The vendor's words seemed to have been formed of spittle and dust. So curious was the sound of his voice that Clint imagined the words sliding like slugs out of the stringy-haired man's mouth.

"Whattya got?" Clint asked. He stared pointedly at the white cargo van parked behind the vendor.

"Everything you knew existed and a lot more that you didn't. We just need to find what's right for you."

Clint narrowed his eyes and tried to figure out if the old guy was yanking his chain. Why was the table empty?

"You collect bootlegs, correct?" the vendor asked.

"I love 'em. Got hundreds," Clint admitted. "Reel to reel, vinyl, compact discs. I'm working on transferring everything onto a thirty gigabyte flash drive."

"And what are your favorites?" The vendor tented his fingers together and leaned forward in a pose of concentration.

"My favorite bootlegs don't have a lot in common musically," Clint said. "The Metallica and GNR show in August of '92 is kickass. First Hetfield almost turns into a crispy critter, then Guns walk off and the fans riot."

The vendor nodded appreciatively. Emboldened, Clint continued. "The best GNR bootleg is from the spring of '88 at the Monsters of Rock Festival at Castle Donington. At the beginning of their set one hundred thousand fans surged forward and..." Clint licked his lips, suddenly self-conscious.

"And two fans were trampled to death." The vendor surprised Clint by saying.

"Yeah. That's right. But you can't really tell when it happens. It's not obvious, but you know it happens."

The stringy-haired vendor stuck out a hand. "Name's Mister Mojo."

"Clint Porter." He grabbed the grinning mans' cold appendage and gave it a squeeze. Clint heard the vendor's knuckles crack and involuntarily jerked his own sweating palm back to his side.

"Other favorites?" Mojo prompted. Clint scuffed a shoe against the asphalt and bit his lower lip. "The Who at Riverfront Coliseum in Cincinnati on December 3rd 1979 is good but you don't hear any of the important parts."

"Eleven souls for rock n' roll." The vendor nodded thoughtfully. "But it all happened in the stampede for seats before the show."

"Right. But I've got several different bootlegs from the Altamont Speedway Festival and you can hear the shit going down in those." Clint felt goose bumps rise on his skin. His lungs rattled and he fought back a cough. "And when the bikers cut loose on that guy in the front row, and Mick is yellin' for the crowd to be cool, that's an intense listening experience."

"Was there a bootleg of the Great White show at The Station from February of 2003?" Mojo wondered aloud.

"Shit, yes!" Clint felt his face flushing. He'd listened to the audio from that show so many times he'd lost count. The vendor didn't seem to be judging him. *May as well go for broke.*

"Someone dropped their mini-cassette recorder when they ran and a fireman sold the tape on the black market," Clint revealed. "I've got a second generation copy. I put on my headphones and listen to it when I grill."

The vendor cackled and Clint giggled self-consciously. Some browsers in the next booth cast disapproving looks their direction. Mojo paid them no mind. Clint fumbled in his fanny pack for his inhaler and fired two puffs into his lungs.

"I like your style," the old vendor announced. "I have a series of bootlegs that you might be very interested in."

Clint concentrated on regulating his breathing and waited for Mr. Mojo to continue. The skies overhead had darkened under the threat of an afternoon thunderstorm and the vendor's chair seemed to have drawn back toward the back door of the white van.

The vendor named his price. It was just enough green for Clint to know he'd be getting something worthwhile.

Mojo held out his hand and Clint deposited several bills in the other man's palm.

"I'm going to give you a copy of the first installment in a series of bootleg recordings. If you enjoy it, come visit me again." The vendor stood and shook the dirty gray hair from his shoulders. His bony legs creaked inside the black leather pants he wore. Clint's nostrils twitched and he tried to ignore the smell. Mojo's outfit desperately needed to be washed...or burned. The old man clambered into the back of the shadowy van.

Clint tried to see what the vendor had stored inside but could make out nothing. The interior seemed incredibly dark, even taking into account the rapidly approaching storm. Clint shoved his hands in his pockets and chewed on his bottom lip. The wind began to pluck at his ponytail and throw grit in his eyes.

The other vendors were rapidly tearing down their booths and most of the people browsing had already returned to their vehicles. The first bolt of lightning crackled across the sky over his head and Clint hunched his neck between his shoulders as ice cold drops began to slap against his skin. He wanted to pound on the back of the van door. Finally Mojo emerged and handed him a small flat white box. The box obviously held an old tape reel.

"This is an extraordinary listening experience that I am allowing you to partake of," the vendor declared as Clint shoved his small parcel into hiding under his shirt. "After you've listened to it, come back and we'll talk about the complete set."

Clint nodded hurriedly. "Who's the band?"

Mr. Mojo smirked, "Well buddy, it ain't no rock show!"

Baffled, Clint stared at the vendor. Finally he asked, "Will you be here next weekend?" A lightning bolt reflected in Mojo's watery eyes and he nodded.

Clint spun on his heel and jogged awkwardly toward his car. Once inside, he breathed in two more puffs from his inhaler and draped himself helplessly over his steering wheel until his ragged breathing gradually returned to its usual mild wheeze. The rain cascaded down. Clint started the car, turned his headlights on and put the windshield wipers to work. Across the parking lot, Mr. Mojo and his unassuming white van had disappeared into the storm.

#

The white box bore no markings and the plastic reel inside was wrapped in a greasy leaf of yellowed notebook paper. Clint gingerly removed the paper wrapping and gazed at his prize. He wondered if he was about to hear the first recordings of someone who would go on to achieve fame or if he would hear the final recording made by an aging star before they died.

Clint approached his reel to reel machine and placed his recent purchase on the left reel knob. He pulled the tape through the spoolers and across the tape heads. A thrill of anticipation coursed through him as he wound the tape onto the take-up spool and adjusted the tension of the tape. Clint toggled to 7 1/2 inches per second, the more dynamic speed for live recordings. Since he didn't have speakers hooked up to the old reel to reel machine, he plugged his best pair of headphones into the front of the unit instead. He stabbed the playback button with his index finger and closed his eyes.

Chipmunks chattered in his ears. What was this shit? Some unreleased recordings from Ross Bagnasarian?

The higher voiced chipmunk was squealing now. Sounds like they're arguing. Realization dawned in Clint's brain and he flipped the speed toggle back to 3 3/4 inches per second. The squealing chipmunk voice became the moaning of an old woman.

"Just take my money and leave me be!" her disembodied voice quavered.

Clint felt his skin break out in goose bumps. This was no rock concert.

"I don't want your money," a male voice replied. "I want to do something."

"Sweet Jesus! Somebody help!"

To Clint the woman could have been around sixty, but her smoker's voice may have been skewing the numbers. The man's age was harder to pin down.

"The more you fuss the more this will hurt," the man warned. "Let's get you out of your bathrobe."

Scuffling sounds escalated into a the crash of what sounded like a lamp falling and breaking. Muffled fleshy thuds moved from his right ear to his left and Clint could almost see the woman scrambling across the floor on her hands and knees. The man's footfalls covered the room in a second. The sound of the man pouncing on the woman thundered in Clint's ears. The woman groaned but no longer seemed to be putting up a fight.

A few moments passed and then he heard the guy grunting with pleasure. Clint had a pretty clear idea of what was happening, but he heard sounds coming from the woman too. Not moaning exactly. Gagging? Choking?

Clint realized he was hearing two crimes happen simultaneously and suddenly found it hard to breathe. He fumbled for the inhaler and released a burst into his lungs. Clint heard his own gasp for air, the attacker's groan of pleasure and the woman's death rattle simultaneously.

Clint heard footsteps approaching and spun around, but the room was empty. The footsteps had come from the tape. The attacker now stood in front of the recording device. His breathing came in labored gasps.

"I used the cord from her bathrobe. She's the first. It was good but something was lacking. Maybe it will come to me during playback."

A metallic click ended the events. A slight hiss was the only sound as the rest of the reel unspooled. Clint shakily removed the headphones and waddled to his recliner. It was only after he'd sunk into it that he became aware of his subsiding erection and the clammy wetness in his shorts.

#

"Who is he?" Clint asked the vendor the next weekend.

"If you keep listening you'll hear clues," Mr. Mojo replied. "The entire series is well worth both your time and money."

The table before the vendor once again stood empty. Clint's eyes kept straying to the van. "How many tapes are there total?"

"Seven."

"How much?" Clint found it hard to make eye contact with the bootleg vendor. Mojo mentioned a sum double what he had asked for the week prior. Clint grabbed his wallet. "That's very reasonable."

"That's the cost for the next installment only," the old man warned.

Clint counted his cash, found that he had just enough, and handed it across the table. Mojo entered the pitch black confines of his van and stayed for several minutes. Clint found himself imagining the old man making his way through an endless maze of shelves, seeking out the proper reel from within a vast warehouse of darkness and dust. He glanced around self-consciously. None of the other customers ever seemed to stop by this table. And why should they? It stood empty and apart from the other vendors.

Clint returned his focus to the old man as he emerged from the van once again holding only a simple white box.

"See you next weekend." The stringy-haired vendor phrased this not as a question, Clint realized, but as a statement.

#

Clint's stomach clenched as he wound the second tape through the machine and pressed play. He heard footsteps creaking up a flight of stairs and knuckles rapping on a door. A muffled inquiry that Clint couldn't make out came next and the man replied, "Building maintenance, ma'am."

The door creaked open, and the woman's voice was clearer now. "I didn't place a call; there's nothing the matter." This woman sounded even older than the first one.

"I'm sorry to inconvenience you, ma'am. The apartment below yours has water dripping down in their kitchen from the ceiling. Would you mind if I took a quick look under your sink to make sure that isn't where the leak is coming from?"

The elderly woman murmured an exclamation, as if fearful of unwittingly being the culprit of the problem, and invited him in.

"I'll put my box of tools here on the counter," the man said. "And then I'm going to do something." Clint heard—or maybe he imagined—the sound of a zipper.

"Stop that!" the elderly woman demanded. "You take that out in the bathroom, not here!"

"Where I take it out and where I put it in are both entirely my decision," the man patiently explained. Clint heard him lunge at the woman. She uttered a high-pitched scream that choked off abruptly. Then victim apparently crashed to the floor. Clint heard the attacker cursing in surprise. Then it sounded like he retreated a few steps. The woman continued to groan but the man said nothing. Clint furrowed his brows in confusion. Then the man's footsteps approached the counter.

"I think she's having a heart attack," the voice confided. "Happened right when I grabbed her." The man paused and Clint imagined him looking back over his shoulder at the old woman. "I was going to choke her with my bare hands while I did it to her, to see if that would make it more rewarding. The cord from the bathrobe really didn't work for me. But she dropped like a sack of potatoes. "

Another pause, the old woman groaning, then: "This isn't really my scene, I'm gonna split." The metallic click came next. Clint tossed his headphones aside and let the tape unspool.

Clint wondered at the identity of the man. Someone famous or an unknown? There were seven in the series, according to the bootleg vendor. The first one had been an intense listening experience, even upon repeated listening. The second one felt like a letdown in comparison. But Clint knew the importance of listening to the entire series in sequence. He wanted to hear everything in context.

And if he wanted to hear any more in the series, he realized he would have to make a trip to his bank or the nearest cash machine.

#

Clint planned ahead and brought double the amount that he paid for the second bootleg. Mojo saw him coming and crawled into the van to retrieve the third reel in the series.

"He hits his stride with this performance," the old man proclaimed. "There are screams—though not from the audience—and some applause at the end." The seedy vendor, still wearing the same outfit as the previous two weekends, favored Clint with a leer that showcased a row of crooked black teeth and chuckled.

Clint ran two red lights in his hurry to return home.

#

Once again, the killer posed as a maintenance man to successfully gain entry and the victim again sounded old enough to easily be someone's grandmother.

"I'm going to do something," the attacker said again before he grabbed the woman. When the attacker demanded the victim remove her nylon stockings, Clint took notice. The woman sobbed and began reciting the Lord's Prayer as her attacker moved in. Her prayer quickly turned to screams and Clint knew as surely as if he were there that the man had wrapped the nylons around the old woman's neck. Her cries became more guttural and choked as the man apparently twisted them around his fist.

Before long Clint heard a long groan pleasure. "Goddamn!" The killer enthused. Clint heard the man panting and the sound of the woman being dropped unceremoniously to the floor. Alone in the room, the killer applauded. Then the panting man approached the reel to reel machine to make his customary report.

"The boys ain't even got a winning record so far this season. 34 wins to 40 losses? Sonuva bitch. That old broad kicked the bucket on me last night and our boys kicked the bucket against the Angels two nights running. I needed cheering up. So I paid a visit to someone right away instead of waiting."

Clint adjusted his trousers, found his enjoyment of the recording had equaled that of the attacker's and exhaled a ragged breath. The killer rambled on:

"Nylons are the way to go from now on for sure. Loop them over their head and around my fist. If I take 'em from behind and standing up, they can't scratch me." The man sounded like he was reciting the recipe for a new favorite dish. "Then, the closer they get to unconsciousness, the more limp their bodies get and the more pressure they put on the stockings around their neck 'cause they're wanting to fall. If I keep twisting the extra fabric around my fist, gravity does all the work and when I'm done, I just drop 'em and walk away."

#

The events on the tape of the fourth reel played out similar to the previous recording, except that woman whimpered rather than prayed and the killer managed to drag out the proceedings a few minutes longer.

At the end, the man confided smugly, "I'm no dummy. I don't take off the plastic gloves until I get home. I'll never be caught; I might even be a genius."

This was followed by a short chortle cut off by a metallic click.

Clint let the tape unspool and went to check the status of his online auctions. He had to own the entire series but needed three more to complete the set, and the price kept doubling every time. After emptying his meager savings, he'd taken to selling his most rare and sought-after bootlegs online to raise the cash. Clint felt like a junkie craving his next fix, but what an astonishingly rewarding fix it was.

#

"Figure it out yet?" Mojo asked as Clint shuffled up the next weekend.

"Not yet, but I will." Clint said with more desire than conviction.

"The answer's right in front of your nose, friend!" The old man chided him. "Pay attention to the rambling he does at the end of this tape and you'll have it."

#

Clint listened to the fifth reel with mounting excitement. This time the man had more trouble than usual talking his way into the elderly woman's apartment, but he got in just the same. By now the killer had mastered his strangulation technique. Also his habit of uttering the phrase 'I'm going to do something now,' had created in Clint a Pavlovian response. It was at this moment that he now became sexually excited during the recordings.

This time Clint and the killer cried out in unison. After he heard the killer drop the woman to the floor—shag carpet this time, judging by the soft thump—Clint leaned in like a co-conspirator to hear the killer's thoughts.

"Had to wait longer than I wanted to for this one. Newspapers are all over this, especially the friggin' Herald. Cops telling everyone not to open the door to strangers. I had so many strikeouts it was pathetic. Speaking of strikeouts, the boys had a five game win streak going against the Indians and Orioles and what do they do? Back to their old losing ways. Three straight losses to the Twins and now they're 58 and 67. They ain't even gonna be in the Pennant Race."

Clint realized he was shaking his head sympathetically and stopped. It almost felt as if the killer and he had formed an intimate bond of friendship. The voice on the tape continued.

"If I didn't have this as an outlet to blow off steam, I don't know what I'd do. Y'know this morning I pulled a pair of red socks out of my drawer and was so pissed I threw them in the trash? Jesus!"

The metallic click came and Clint stood staring at the tape reel. The slight hiss matched his wheezing and he absentmindedly reached for his inhaler.

Red socks? Could it be? Clint needed to check on his latest auctions anyway but first he wanted to look something up.

#

"Is it the B—" Clint began to say the next weekend once he'd reached Mojo's table. The old man raised his palm in warning and Clint chose his words more carefully. "The bootleg recordings that I've been purchasing were all recorded in Boston, correct?"

The vendor nodded and leered in approval.

"But why are there only seven? When I looked him up on the Internet, I counted thirteen, uh, events."

Mojo made a face like he'd just discovered a bloody fingernail in his dinner salad.

"With one exception, the entire 'second phase' attributed to this individual was performed by copycats. Would you waste your money on cover bands and tribute concerts? Of course not." The stringy-haired vendor folded his arms and leaned back in his canvas chair. The beating sun had softened the asphalt and heat waves radiated upward in all directions. Clint did his best not to react to the stench emanating from the old man. He thought it smelled like something had died.

The vendor's eyes narrowed and Clint flushed guiltily. The old man stood up and Clint involuntarily took a step back.

"You have enough cash for today's transaction?"

At first Clint was so relieved he couldn't speak, but he finally sputtered an affirmative response and dug in his fanny pack for the wad of cash he'd raised by selling off most of his collection.

Mr. Mojo disappeared into the back of his van. Clint again imagined the vendor shuffling through miles of moldering shelves in some mystical cavernous warehouse. When the vendor emerged from the inky interior of the van, Clint was surprised to see him carrying not one but two small white boxes.

"Bootleg recordings six and seven," the old man announced.

"But I didn't bring enough--" Clint began.

"It's on the house. You're one of my most loyal customers."

"Thanks a lot, really."

"A word of advice however," the man leaned forward as he spoke and Clint automatically bent to listen. "Listen to number six whenever you like. Do NOT however, under any circumstances, listen to the seventh tape until 372 days after listening to number six." Clint stared at the other man blankly. "The seventh event takes place exactly 372 days after the sixth. I am offering the final installment in the series completely free of charge. This saves you a large sum of cash. In return for this favor I only ask that you wait the specified amount before listening. Fair enough?"

"Sure," Clint replied automatically. Mojo handed him the pair of reels ensconced in their boxes like mummies in sarcophagi. Clint turned and began to shuffle to his car. Something occurred to him and he stopped.

"What happens if I don't wait?" He turned all the way around but the canvas chair sat empty. Other customers browsing had looked up and were now staring at Clint with varying degrees of curiosity. Feeling suddenly self-conscious, he fled to his car and drove away.

#

The sixth tape in the series was everything he hoped it would be. The man had to work to talk his way into the elderly woman's apartment. The strangler stretched out the period before the attack by pretending to fiddle with her window-mounted air conditioner and then took his time assaulting the woman and toying with her before ending her life.

The tape ran longer than any of the others in the series and after events had reached their crescendo, Clint found himself applauding and sobbing simultaneously.

Clint ached to tell somebody, but knew he couldn't. Who would believe he had bootleg recordings of the crimes of one of the most notorious serial killers in US history? And who would he share them with anyway? This man had become his de facto friend and confidant. He relished listening to the exploits and ramblings of the strangler. He wished there were more than seven reels.

#

Clint didn't make it 372 days. He made it seven.

Force of habit and the final reel's tempting presence proved too much for Clint's weak will. He *tried* to keep his promise. Clint spent all morning and afternoon listening to the other six in the series. Then he fixed a bachelor's lunch of tomato soup and toast which he gobbled standing at the kitchen counter. When the temptation became too much he fled the house.

He stopped by the flea market but discovered that Mr. Mojo hadn't set up that day. Clint returned home feeling a sense of relief. Somehow not seeing the bootleg vendor gave him a sense of liberation. Clint felt better about listening to the last reel in the series without reprisals from the old man.

His heart pounded with excitement as Clint placed the final reel on the knob. He ceremoniously pulled the tape through the spoolers and across the tape heads, wound the tape onto the take-up spool and adjusted the tension of the tape. Clint placed the headphones over his ears, pressed the playback button and closed his eyes.

"This is a reunion of sorts," announced the man who had killed six times before. "I'm nearing the apartment of a woman who wouldn't let me in last year when everyone in the city was talking about me." In the background, Clint heard an elevator chime. When the man on the tape resumed it was in a much quieter tone. "Copycats all over this city are trying to imitate me and it's really pissing me off. Young women getting raped, old women getting stabbed, and the cops and papers go and blame everything on me. As if I don't have any standards! So I decided to come out of retirement to show the cops how I do MY thing. Then maybe they'll realize I'm not responsible for all this other stuff they're pinning on me."

Silence reigned as the killer presumably reached his destination. Clint heard knuckles rapping on wood.

"Yes?"

"Ma'am, my name is Eric. I'm visiting my aunt down the hall and I thought you should know you've left your keys hanging in your door lock." This was a new variation Clint had never heard and he grinned at the clever misdirection.

The old woman instinctively took the bait and Clint heard the door open so the woman could retrieve her keys. Based on the fleshy smack he heard next, Clint surmised that the killer had struck the woman and forced her back into the room. The door slammed and the man struck again and dragged his victim to the floor.

"Oh don't do that," the elderly woman kept pleading but Clint knew her begging would be of no use.

"I'm keeping one of your stockings in case I need to use it later," the killer explained. "Now, I'm going to do something."

His operation ran as smooth and deadly as ever. Everything went exactly as Clint knew it would. He closed his eyes and reveled in the depravity, cherishing the bond between performer and listener.

"Nobody does it like I do, Clint."

This jarred him from his reverie. The killer had spoken his name. Clint wanted to run but his shoes felt glued to the linoleum. He couldn't even summon up the will to press stop. Clint became aware of a figure approaching from behind but couldn't turn to face him. His body shook with spasms of fear. He could hardly breathe.

"Shoulda followed the rules." The voice on the tape was the unmistakable spittle and dust voice of Mr. Mojo. The room suddenly reeked with the fetid odor of the old man. "I gave you a hoot of warning but you didn't listen. You took the gift I gave you and tarnished it. You sullied the waters of my creation with your lack of restraint."

Clint gaped. He shook his head. It couldn't be.

"I saw you looking for me at the flea market. I knew you'd grown weak already. I followed you home."

The seedy old man flew into action, knocking the headphones from Clint's head and wrapping a nylon stocking around his neck in one whirlwind motion. Clint felt more ashamed than afraid, like a bootlegger busted by his favorite musician.

Clint, still frozen in Mojo's spell, gagged and wheezed as the killer tightened the fabric around his neck. He felt his throat constricting and heard the creak of his windpipe collapsing. Having been asthmatic his entire life, Clint recognized the suffocating feeling that scorched his lungs.

But then Mojo leered and yanked at his trousers, and the reality of the situation hit Clint full force. This would be much more than a harsh warning; this would be a full performance.

THE BIGGIN HILL DUEL

In dictating to the brass cylinders the cases that illustrate the remarkable deductive abilities of my friend Herbert Krane, I have always presented the narratives in a straightforward and factual nature. I never endeavor to sensationalize any of our exploits and I am sure the recordings will bear witness to the truth in this assertion. It is, however, difficult to entirely separate the sensational aspects from the criminal in this particular case. With a disclaimer thusly given, I will now consult my notes and reveal to you an exceedingly peculiar set of circumstances which not only caused one life to end prematurely, but broke a young woman's heart as well.

It was a scorching hot day in mid-July. Rain had not fallen in weeks, and the rainmakers had all been grounded thanks to the petrol shortage. Kater Street shimmered in the yellow sun. Krane lay sprawled upon a sofa. He had dispensed with any attempt at repairing our domestic assistant. There was a catch in the gears in her left elbow which caused that arm to move with spastic jerks. We found it hard to enjoy our customary whiskey and sodas before bed when half the liquid had splashed out onto the serving tray during her approach. We'd taken to living rustically and pouring our own drinks until the necessary repairs could be made.

"The heat plays havoc with the fine-tuning of the gears," Krane had groused. Instead he was examining a letter which he had received by special delivery earlier that morning. I busied myself with some minor correspondence at the desk in the corner.

"It has always seemed to me a most preposterous means of settling a dispute," Krane announced, as if we had been conversing. I pushed my papers aside and turned to my friend.

"What is?" I asked.

"Dueling." Krane sat up and raised the letter he'd been reading. "Have you had the opportunity to examine this morning's paper, Grant?"

I had skimmed the paper, so I nodded in assent.

"Did you take particular note of the brief story on page three, two thirds of the way down the page in the far left column?"

"Good heavens, Krane; I hardly know," I blurted. "What was the nature of the article?"

Krane arose and, sighing at my apparent thick-headedness, picked up the paper folded on the end table. He tossed it in my direction. "Perhaps another perusal would allow us to continue our conversation."

I felt piqued by my friend's chaffing attitude, but dismissed it as a product of the oppressive heat. I picked up the paper he had thrown to me, and read the item indicated. It was headed "Body Found in Park" and read:

> *The body of Denis Evans was found yesterday morning near Biggin Hill in Bromley. Authorities from New Scotland Yard have revealed that the body, discovered by a groundskeeper, suffered a single gunshot wound to the head. Evans was pronounced dead at the scene. The authorities believe Evans may have been involved in a duel and are currently seeking leads. No further information is available at this time.*

I waited for an update to scroll across the page but seeing none I set the paper aside and looked up expectantly at Krane.

"I received this paper letter via special delivery this morning," he said, holding up the note he had recently been absorbed in.

"Let me deduce who has written it," I interjected. "I see cheap paper, and the hurried scrawls of an antique ink pen. Even from across the room I can tell that the letter's author harbors feelings of both reverence and—dare I say it—desire for at least half of the present occupants of this address. Therefore, the letter must have come from a female admirer."

Krane gazed at me steadily. I snickered at my own jest. His brows furrowed in disapproval, but the corners of his mouth twitched slightly as if he were holding back a smile.

"The letter is from an Inspector Crittenden," Krane revealed. "He has solicited my assistance in the case you have just read."

"I see."

"I plan to leave shortly to meet the inspector at the scene of the crime," Krane continued. "Would you care to accompany me?"

"It is such a hot day and I have to catch up on my correspondence," I began. Krane held up a hand.

"Don't make me beg, Grant," he chided me lightly. "You have proven the worth of your companionship on numerous similar occasions."

I searched his face for some trace of mockery but found none. Finally I rose and followed Krane out the door.

A replica hansom cab was waiting for us as we exited Krane's quarters and we immediately climbed aboard. Gears engaged, hidden clockwork relays turned, and we jolted on our way. Steam issued from the mechanical horses' nostrils. The journey was a predominantly silent one as we each dealt with the oppressive heat in our own way. I believe my past law enforcement service in Australia gave me a slight advantage. I sat fairly comfortably, mopping my brow only occasionally. Krane wilted beside me, his eyes closed.

At last we arrived at Biggin Hill. The weather was slightly cooler in this southern borough. I don't know if it was the drop to a more favorable temperature or the impending examination of the scene that revived Krane, but he dropped from the cab with newfound alacrity.

We descended a gentle slope of grass toward an imposing oak. A stocky man who I took to be Inspector Crittenden stood under the vast shade of the tree. He stepped forward as we approached.

"Herbert Krane? It is my pleasure to make your acquaintance," the man made a small bow and held out his hand. "I am Inspector Crittenden of New Scotland Yard."

Krane took the proffered hand and looked around distractedly. Crittenden then turned to me. "You must be Kendrick Grant," he said, "A pleasure, sir."

"Thank you," I said and we shook hands. The inspector's grip was viselike. I wondered if he'd undergone some internal mechanical enhancements.

"Where was the late Mr. Evans employed?" Krane asked.

"He clerked and apprenticed at a haberdashery," Crittenden revealed. "An *authentic* haberdashery. We've already visited his employer. The fellow was shocked, couldn't believe what has happened."

Krane pursed his lips, "So he hadn't worked there long enough to be a victim of the sickness."

The inspector shook his head. "The owner exhibited a bit of mental instability, but I am certain it was more affection on his part than anything. Haberdasher's Disease takes time; one does not earn it overnight."

"Of course," Krane nodded. He turned and wandered toward a spot approximately two meters from the oak and crouched down. Crittenden hurried over to join him and I followed suit at a leisurely pace.

"I see you have already discerned where the body was found Mr. Krane," Crittenden said. "As I wrote in my letter, two pistols were found at the scene. One was still clutched in the victim's hand, the other lay less than a meter away."

Krane scanned the ground in all directions. "Was the victim right or left-handed?"

"The pistol was gripped in his left hand, if that's what you're asking."

"It's not," Krane replied. "But it does lead to my next question: where did the bullet enter Evans' skull?"

"The right eye socket, near the bridge of the nose."

Krane had stood back up. "Were both weapons discharged?"

"Yes," Crittenden responded promptly.

"Were both slugs recovered?"

"One was retrieved from inside the victim, of course. It successfully dispensed its vial of acid. We have not recovered the other slug, however," the inspector admitted. "We surmise the shot went wild and could be anywhere." He made a sweeping gesture over the vast expanse of brown grass surrounding us.

"It would be prudent to locate the slug before any children discover it," I interjected. "If the acid vial has not shattered, a further tragedy could yet unfold."

Krane forgave me for stating the obvious by ignoring my comment. "Would you humor us by walking through the events as the authorities believe they unfolded?" Krane asked Crittenden.

"Certainly. We believe that Evans and another man met here by prearrangement. One of them brought a wooden box that housed the two pistols; probably Evans since the items were left behind when the killer fled."

Crittenden paused, waiting for Krane to make a judgment on this statement. When my friend only gazed up at the sky, the inspector continued.

"We believe the men stood back to back as is customary in a duel and walked their twenty paces. Both men turned and fired. Evans' bullet missed its mark while his assailant's bullet flew true. Evans fell to the ground. His killer approached the body and, upon finding him dead, tossed away his pistol and fled the scene."

Krane looked at me. "What do you make of it Grant?"

"Sounds like a solid appraisal of the events," I allowed.

"And yet only one sentence the Inspector uttered is true; at least in a literal sense."

Crittenden gaped at Krane. His jaw hung open for so long that I had to resist the urge to reach out a hand and gently close it.

"B-b-but Mr. Krane, h-h-how...?" Inspector Crittenden reminded me of a mechanical minstrel with a scratched song cylinder.

"You said 'Evans fell to the ground.' In that statement you are correct." Krane strode about halfway back to our waiting hansom cab and knelt. "But see here."

Inspector Crittenden knelt beside Krane while I stationed myself between them and looked over their shoulders. Krane dug with his fingers into the sun-baked ground. In moments he withdrew a misshapen chunk of lead. Tiny shards of glass protruded from the tip. The acid had been safely absorbed into the soil.

"The second slug." My friend offered it to Crittenden. Looking dubious, the inspector took it, examined it briefly, and then made it disappear into a special pocket.

Krane stood and brushed loose brown grass from his knees. "I believe that Evans was taken by surprise and shot pointblank. With that in mind, it was easy to deduce that when the fatal bullet struck him, his fingers clenched reflexively and he pulled the trigger while the gun was still pointed in the air."

"But how the deuce did you know where the slug would have landed?" Crittenden sputtered. "Was it a mathematical formula of trajectory?"

"It could have been, but not this time. I simply felt the hole in the ground under my sole as we approached you."

"You just happened to step on the hole." The inspector looked unconvinced.

"Sometimes luck factors in," Krane replied blandly. Crittenden and I exchanged questioning glances.

"Now then, I believe I have solved the case but should like to examine the quarters of the deceased if possible. There are a few particulars that I am still in the dark about."

Crittenden grabbed Krane by the shoulders. "Good Heavens, man! You know where the shooter is, then?"

"Beyond your reach, I'm afraid," Krane said soberly. "Now then, may we visit Evans' quarters?"

"Yes of course," Crittenden replied, "But—"

"In due time, Inspector." Krane turned and strode toward our gently rumbling hansom replica. "In due time."

The drive to Lewisham from adjacent Bromley was considerably shorter than our first trip of the day. Krane had ordered our hansom driver to follow Inspector

Crittenden's conveyance and settled back in his seat. I looked at passing scenery and was left alone with my thoughts. It was only as we approached the former residence of the late Mr. Evans that Krane roused himself.

"Now then Grant, we shall have a firsthand look at how a singular man like Denis Evans lived." Krane's eyes glittered with enthusiasm that I confess I could not match. The building itself looked similar to the others in the area, and—except for the fact that Evans had perished in a duel—I could ascertain nothing remarkable about the man or his situation.

Kranc and I disembarked and strode toward Inspector Crittenden who was already standing at the foot of the building's front steps. Inside, on the first floor, we found the dwelling of the building's superintendent. The inspector rapped sharply on the door, which quickly swung open to reveal a wispy little man with disheveled white hair and a pince-nez clipped to the bridge of a surprisingly bold nose.

Inspector Crittenden introduced himself and received an introduction in turn. The little superintendent's name was Eustace Lyons.

"We would like to examine the residence of Denis Evans," Crittenden said.

"Yes of course," Mr. Lyons acquiesced. "He's in two-oh-four. *Was*, I should say. If you gentlemen will follow me..."

Lyons led the way to the moving stairs, followed by Crittenden and then Krane. I brought up the rear. The little man threw a lever. Hidden wheels turned and gears engaged. The ascent was a remarkably smooth one which is not always the case in these poorer neighborhoods.

"How long had Mr. Evans been a tenant?" Krane asked the white-haired man above the hum of machinery.

"I'd say two years, give or take a month," Lyons responded.

"Did you know him well?"

"I knew him well enough to nod hello whenever I saw him," the superintendent said. "He was a pleasant fellow most days, although he had his quiet moments as well."

"Oh?"

"You know how young clerks sometimes are," Lyons confided. "One day they seem like they're on top of the world, the next it's as if they believe everyone is out to get them."

"That's the way it was with Evans then?" Crittenden asked.

"Yes, you never knew if he was running hot or cold. Always very courtly in his manners, however. He was a bit old fashioned in that regard." Lyons had stopped before the outer door of the apartment Evans had rented. He withdrew a gold key, inserted it into the lock and turned it. The outer door slid into the wall revealing the apartment's vault door. The superintendent twisted the knob right, left, and right as he consulted a series of numbers displayed on tiny squares of paper under the glass of a converted timepiece. The ingenuity of his invention convinced me the little landlord was also to thank for the perfect operation of the moving stairs. A hollow thud told us the apartment was unlocked. Lyons pressed his palm against the door and made as if to enter but Krane stopped him with a hand on the shoulder.

"I should prefer to enter first," my friend confided gravely.

The smaller man looked affronted and opened his mouth to reply but Krane spoke first. "For investigative purposes, of course. I have reason to believe the killer may have been on the premises recently."

The superintendent jerked backward in such surprise that the pince nez popped off his nose. Inspector Crittenden also cast a startled look in Krane's direction. Lyons kept my attention. His pince nez swung from its black ribbon like a man in a noose. This sobering image returned my thoughts immediately returned to the matter at hand.

Krane had already entered Evans' former quarters. I could see his silhouette outlined in the window as he moved about the interior. Krane disappeared down a short hall, which presumably led to sleeping quarters and the bath. Moments later he returned to the door.

"It is just as I suspected." Krane stood aside and we all entered. The young bachelor was by turns tidy and slovenly. Dirty clothing had been thrown haphazardly across the floor in the sitting room, while in the bedroom all the clothing hung on hangers, and looked neatly pressed. Polished black shoes and dirty brown boots stood side by side in the tiny foyer. The bed was neatly made, yet the couch in the sitting room sat in disarray. I thought this odd and after we had perused the rooms, I approached my friend. He gave me an expectant smile.

"What do you make of it, Grant?"

"It looks as if two people lived here," I volunteered. The wispy little superintendent shook his head as if to argue, but Inspector Crittenden nodded, stroking his chin thoughtfully.

"On what do you base this assessment?"

"I base it on the clothing and other household items." I indicated some of them with a wave of my hand. "Some are put in their proper places while others are strewn about carelessly."

"Did any of you gentlemen happen to notice the pictograph on that wall?" Krane pointed.

We all turned and moved in for closer examination. The framed pictograph showed a rather beautiful young woman turning and gazing precociously at the camera. Her dark hair hung in ringlets and she flashed a marvelous smile and blinked long eyelashes. She looked to me like a woman who could steal hearts on a whim. As we watched the scene began again. I confess I nearly fell in love all over again as she turned her gaze upon the camera again. After the third time, I tore myself away and turned back to Krane.

"Am I correct in my assessment that this young lady could be considered quite attractive?" Krane asked us. We all nodded and chorused our assent.

"Did any of you look close enough to make out the inscription?" Krane pressed.

Lyons and I both turned back to the photograph in surprise but Inspector Crittenden nodded. I removed the pictograph from the wall and held it closer to the light shining in from the window for better viewing.

"*For Denis and Ralph, with all my love, Charlotte.*" I read aloud.

"Good heavens," Lyons exclaimed. "A proclamation of love directed at two men?"

"Perhaps it is just a friendly term of endearment," I suggested. "They may all be old school chums."

"Regardless, we now have a solid lead on a suspect," Crittenden said.

I nodded and passed the pictograph to the inspector.

"But I never saw anyone other than Evans enter or leave this apartment," Lyons attested. "Who was this 'Ralph'? How could he have been staying here without my knowledge?"

"Ralph could have been here with precious few knowing about it," Krane declared. "I suspect Charlotte and Denis may have been the only two persons aware of Ralph's presence."

"Then we must make every effort to locate the woman in the pictograph," Inspector Crittenden said, "Perhaps she knows the whereabouts of the mysterious Ralph. I believe he could very easily have been the second participant in the duel."

"I agree with the inspector in that we must seek out this young lady, albeit with a different purpose in mind." Krane turned to the inspector. "How soon can you have men making inquiries?"

"Within the hour," Crittenden announced after a moment's consideration. He had turned the pictograph over and was examining the back. "We can start with the shop where the pictograph was taken.

"Capital! Let's have some fresh air then," Krane replied. He strode out of the room and disappeared in the direction of the moving stairs. Inspector Crittenden thanked Mr. Lyons for his assistance. I shook the superintendent's hand and followed the inspector outside.

Inspector Crittenden and I found Krane already seated in our cab. The driver had kept the cab running and the mechanical horses had built up full heads of steam. Krane spoke as we approached. "Fourteen blocks south, we passed a small but serviceable-looking eating establishment. Grant and I have breakfasted, but have not eaten since. I, for one, am famished and would make the supposition that Grant is as well."

I nodded in the affirmative and Krane went on. "I wonder if you would be kind enough, Inspector, to notify us with any news on the whereabouts of the lovely Miss Charlotte?"

Inspector Crittenden nodded and Krane gave him the name of the restaurant where he intended us to dine. Crittenden returned to his own conveyance and Krane nodded at our driver who had heard the establishment named and knew its location. Once we were off, I engaged Krane in a bit of light banter on a few meaningless topics. I knew better than to press my companion about the current case. Krane would reveal all in due time.

We had just pushed back our plates from an exceedingly satisfying meal when a panting youth entered the establishment and looked around expectantly. Krane nodded when the newcomer looked our way and he hurried over. "Mr. Herbert Krane?"

My friend nodded. The young man removed his hat. "I sure am honored."

"You needn't be," Krane assured him. "Do you have a dispatch for us?"

"Yes, yes!" the boy replied, as if just remembering. He pulled a small ink-stained cube from his front pocket and placed it carefully on the table. From his other pocket the lad produced a jar of liquid. He unscrewed the lid revealing a brush attached to the underside of the metal. He quickly and carefully applied a fresh coat of ink to the cube and stepped back. Krane glanced at the cube and then held it up for me to read.

Misters Krane and Grant,
   The photographer remembered her immediately. Miss Charlotte Bennett resides at 2—— Altamont Terrace, also in Lewisham. Will meet you there.
                               Inspector Crittenden

"I was looking forward to having a smoke after dinner." Krane sighed resignedly as his long fingers tapped his cigar case. "But I suppose time is of essence."

I took note of the glimmer in his eye and realized that my friend was looking forward to an audience with the newly discovered Miss Bennett.

"Just smoke in the cab on the way," I said and rose to pay the bill. The youth stepped in to retrieve his cube and I compensated him as well.

The driver, a clever fellow born for his type of work, was familiar with the Altamont Terrace address and indicated that it was nearby. Krane and I took our seats and in a matter of minutes our replica hansom arrived at the young woman's residence.

We waited outside for Inspector Crittenden to arrive. Krane continued to smoke placidly while I watched the windows for any sign of movement. The skies had started to darken, but no lamps had been lit within Miss Bennett's dwelling.

I pointed this out to Krane, saying, "Perhaps she is not at home."

"She's home," my companion replied, but would say no more.

After another ten minutes, Crittenden arrived. "I made for New Scotland Yard and had to double back," he explained.

The three of us found ourselves once again at a stranger's door. Inspector Crittenden knocked and we waited. When no one immediately answered, Crittenden rapped harder. Finally a muffled voice came from the darkness within.

"Yes?"

"Miss Charlotte Bennett?" Crittenden inquired.

"Who's calling?"

"Inspector Crittenden of New Scotland Yard. I'd like to ask you a few questions."

The door opened a crack, revealing a bloodshot blue eye which otherwise would have been beautiful if not for the puffiness of recent tears. She appraised us all bleakly.

"What is it that you want, Inspector?" she asked after several moments of silence.

"We came to offer our condolences, my dear lady," Krane surprised me by saying.

Miss Bennett met his gaze. "And who are you?" She still held the door open only a crack.

"Herbert Krane. This is my friend Kendrick Grant," Krane gestured toward me. Her eyes widened briefly in recognition, then narrowed.

"I see you already know my situation. Have you come simply to satisfy your curiosity?"

"We do have some questions," Inspector Crittenden began, but Krane cut him off.

"Our aim, Miss Bennett, is only to put this matter to rest and in so doing, preserving the honor of the man you cared so deeply for."

Her eyes met his and after another pause, her resolve seemed to crumble, and she opened the door wide to admit us into her home. It was small and old-fashioned, but appeared clean and comfortable. Miss Bennett lit a lamp on a small end table and sat down in a nearby chair. Krane perched in the chair opposite her while Inspector Crittenden stood nearby. I lingered near the door where I could more easily see the group.

"How long were you acquainted with Mr. Denis Evans, Miss Bennett?" Krane inquired.

"Over a year. Fifteen months to be more precise."

"Very good," Krane tented his fingers. "And how much time passed before you became aware of Ralph?"

Miss Bennett flushed slightly. "About four months. I'd noticed a change in Denis' moods from time to time but it wasn't until I'd actually been a guest inside his home that I realized his situation."

"And yet you continued the friendship."

"Of course." Miss Bennett raised her chin. "I had begun to care a great deal about Denis."

"And Ralph?"

"Despite their differences, both Ralph and Denis treated me like complete gentlemen. In time, they both professed their love for me."

Inspector Crittenden finally could stand it no more. "You are obviously aware, Miss Bennett, that Mr. Evans lost his life in a duel yesterday morning."

Miss Bennett nodded and blinked away fresh tears.

"We believe this fellow, Ralph, is responsible for the deed," Crittenden pressed. "We know this must be very difficult for you, but he must be brought to justice."

Miss Bennett shrugged her shoulders and gave the inspector a humorless smile.

Crittenden stepped closer and his voice took on an edge. "If you withhold information, Miss Bennett, you will be obstructing the law."

She looked tiredly at Krane. "Do you wish to tell him or should I?"

Krane reached out and took her hand. "Dear lady, you have been through so much."

She lowered her head and bit her trembling bottom lip in an effort to stave off the sobs that now threatened.

Krane looked up and addressed the inspector and myself. "Miss Bennett loved two men within the same body."

Inspector Crittenden scowled, not understanding, but realization dawned upon me and I confess that I gasped aloud. The remarkable situation suddenly became clear and feelings of sympathy rose within me for the girl.

"What the devil are you getting at?" Crittenden finally ejaculated.

"Denis Evans suffered from multiple personalities," Krane explained. "Not quite the madness it was once believed to be, but still a curious medical condition. Grant may have more knowledge upon the subject than I."

I stepped forward. "A contemporary of mine, Dr. Eugene Azam recently wrote a paper concerning a woman he called Felinda X. Dr. Azam is a professor of surgery who has a great interest in hypnotism. While under his care, this Felinda X exhibited three different, distinct personalities. Even more surprising, each personality apparently had no knowledge of the others. Whenever one personality took control, the others experienced periods of amnesia."

"Why, that sounds preposterous!" Inspector Crittenden cried. "A child's fairy tale!"

"Not at all," Krane said with quiet authority. "I will explain more outside." He turned to our hostess. "Miss Bennett, would you like us to summon someone to stay with you and attend to your needs during this difficult time?"

"My mother, Lady Frances Bennett, should be arriving by zeppelin tomorrow," Miss Bennett replied, dabbing at her eyes with a limp handkerchief. "I sent for her this morning after I read the horrible news in the morning edition."

"If that is the case, then let us depart," Krane instructed. "We have intruded upon Miss Bennett for too long."

I glanced at the young lady who, even in her sorrow, looked exquisite. I offered my condolences and followed Krane, who had stood and was ushering the stunned inspector from the room.

Inspector Crittenden kept silent until we were beside our hansom replica, then he blurted, "This is really more than I can swallow, Mr. Krane. I hoped you might discover some overlooked clue, not put forth a sensationalized and ludicrous theory about the case!"

Krane only smiled thinly and raised both hands in a placating gesture. "Give me only a few moments, Inspector, and I will explain myself fully."

Crittenden frowned but nodded.

"I suspected something out of the ordinary immediately upon examining the crime scene," Krane began. "The earth was dry and the grass brown from the heat and lack of rain. The blades broke easily wherever we trod. You and your men stomped most of the grass between the road and the tree, but I was still able to distinguish Mr. Evans' movements. I discerned right away where the unfortunate young man had initially paced under the oak tree, waiting for Ralph to arrive. I saw where Evans turned and counted off his paces, but I could find no corresponding disturbance in the grass of anyone walking in the opposite direction. The grass there was untouched. Moreover, based on the angle Evans took, his adversary—had there been one—could have taken only four or five paces before being obstructed by the large oak tree that stands there. When you described where the slug had entered the victim, I surmised briefly that the shooter was standing right next to the victim when he fired his pistol."

Krane paused and glanced at the inspector, who was now nodding solemnly. I had no trouble visualizing the scene at the base of Biggin Hill as Krane described it, and I'm sure Inspector Crittenden was mentally doing the same. Evans' last moments came to me with startling clarity.

"Evans turned to fire, only to find that his 'opponent' had decided against the gentlemanly approach," Krane continued. "I surmised that 'Ralph' had crept up on him, so to speak, and pulled the trigger from the only range possible."

"Point blank." Crittenden's voice was little more than an awed whisper. He looked up at Krane. "Pray continue."

"There's not much more to tell about the act itself," Krane replied. "The Ralph personality took umbrage to Denis and his interest in Miss Bennett. Although Denis himself may have been the dominant personality, Ralph may well have been the more passionate of the two. They decided on a duel, with the winner free to advance his relationship with Miss Bennett. You've seen the result."

"But Krane," I interjected. "In nearly all documented cases of split or multiple personalities, each personality experiences periods of amnesia, or blackouts, when another side is in control. How in heaven's name did Denis learn of Ralph's presence?"

"Sadly, Miss Bennett is to blame." Krane glanced at her window. "Matters came to a head when she inscribed her pictograph to both personalities. Imagine adjoining rooms. By expressing her affection for both personalities, Miss Bennett threw open the door connecting the two rooms and the tenants got a good look at one another."

"You mean to say...?" Crittenden began.

"Yes. This young woman unconditionally loved and accepted Mr. Evans despite his peculiar condition, but she inadvertently brought about his death by acknowledging both personalities in her proclamation of love."

Crittenden uttered a low oath. I felt my sympathies rising again on behalf of Miss Bennett.

"So in the end, there is no one to be brought to justice," the inspector concluded. "It was a victimless crime."

"Not at all, Inspector." Krane stepped up and settled into our cab. "There was no crime, *but there is a victim*."

Crittenden stepped back and raised one hand in salutation as our driver threw a lever and the mechanical horses sprang forward. Krane slumped back against the seat.

"Dreadful business, that," I volunteered. "But may I congratulate you on your remarkable deductions."

"Thank you, Grant," my companion replied flatly. I could see that familiar melancholy settling upon him. "My findings in this case have left me in a somber and introspective frame of mind. Pray leave me to my thoughts until we have returned to Kater Street."

I settled back and tried to relax, but the hum of the hansom's wheels and the clatter of steel hooves on the cobblestones disturbed my thoughts. The incessant buzzing of the gears and the squeals of steam ejecting from rubber nostrils now reminded me of voices arguing heatedly with one another and the drive proved to be a long and uncomfortable one.

WAITING FOR INSPIRATION

For the first time in weeks, I had time to sit down at my computer and write. The blank screen seemed to gaze at me expectantly. I cracked my knuckles and held my fingertips poised over the keys. *Nothing.* I leaned back and waited for inspiration to strike.

A movement outside my window caught my attention. I turned in time to see a silver disc hovering above the woods behind my house. Something dropped from the craft and landed in my back yard. Even from a distance, I recognized my dog, Furatu. I hurried outside, pausing just long enough to grab the rifle I always kept loaded and leaning beside the door.

In my driveway, I knelt and squeezed off two carefully aimed rounds into a pair of shambling corpses who had wandered too close to the property line. Their heads exploded like watermelons and I was on the move again before their bodies had toppled.

Furatu lay on his side about thirty yards away. I stooped to pick up the rope attached to the drain spout, tied a loop around my waist and went to retrieve my dog.

I lifted Furatu's remains and discovered they were dry and hollow thanks to those bothersome aliens. I swallowed the lump in my throat, tucked his remains under one arm and turned back to the house which—thanks to a curse put on it by the previous owner—had disappeared. I sighed, closed my eyes, and followed the rope with my free hand. It was tough ignoring the ominous slithering and gibbering sounds that trailed me, but I managed.

Once safely inside, I locked the door and carried Furatu downstairs. Inside his cell, my twin brother screamed and threw his shoulder against the heavy wooden door as I passed. I ignored him. I chose a different door farther down the hall, reached out, and pulled a string. The forty watt bulb barely swept the shadows into the corners of the room. I opened the lid of the deep freeze and placed my dearly departed dog inside, right beside Mother. I smiled sadly at both of them for a moment and closed the lid. On impulse I moved to the southeast corner of the room, knelt and felt for the metal ring. The trap door creaked upward and a musty odor invaded my nostrils. I grabbed a flashlight from a nearby shelf and lowered myself into the dank chamber. The beam of light pierced the darkness, illuminating the wine Poe had immortalized. It's not that expensive, but you have to know where to find it. I mentally reminded myself to grab a bottle on the way back up.

I stooped and inched my way down a stone passage until I came to the end of the tunnel where a reinforced steel circle served as a hybrid manhole cover and bank vault door. I pressed one ear to the cover and listened. I staggered to my feet after only a few seconds. My ears burned and I wiped at the blood which now poured from my nose. The prisoner was still inside. I tried not to think about what would happen to the solar system if it were ever to break loose.

I scurried back toward the wine cellar and then climbed up the ladder. I discarded the flashlight, closed the trapdoor and pulled the string, leaving the room in darkness. I realized I'd forgotten the Amontillado, but didn't feel like going back down for it.

My twin brother continued to rave as I passed his cell and I felt a twinge of guilt. I don't remember if he's the Evil Twin or if I am. Best that he stay locked up until I know for sure.

Back upstairs, I peeled off my bloody t-shirt and tossed it onto the pile. The laundry gnomes would take care of my dirty clothes while I slept. As long as they got their customary sacrificial sock, they served obediently. I shrugged into a black dress shirt that had once belonged to a priest who was famous for conducting exorcisms. Or maybe it had belonged to a serial killer. It's so hard to keep track details.

Back in my little office where I do my writing, I was surprised to notice that the sun had set. Daylight had only lasted six hours today. Someone wearing what appeared to be an oversized top hat leapt from tree to tree across my yard, trailing blue flames behind him. I closed the curtains against the distraction. Chains rattled in the attic above me and something uttered a mournful moan. It slowly descended the creaking stairs.

I forced myself to block it all out. No more distractions.

I stared at the computer screen.

I still had no ideas.

I sighed and pushed my chair back. I'll have to try again tomorrow and hope that inspiration strikes.

ACKNOWLEDGMENTS

"Hydrophobia", *Something Dark in the Doorway*, ed. Gregory Miller, Static Movement, 2010; "Tomorrow's Headline", *Night Terrors*, ed. Theresa Dillon, Blood Bound Books, 2010; "Swollen Tick", *Love Kills: My Bloody Valentine*, ed. Jessy Marie Roberts, Pill Hill Press, 2010; "Cold Feet", *Bonded By Blood II: A Romance in Red*, eds. Steven N. Marshall, David Saliba and Wendy Brewer, SNM Horror, 2009; "Bootlegs From Boston" published with the title "Ramblings of the Lunatic", *Bonded By Blood 3: Languish in Lament*, ed. Steven N. Marshall, SNM Horror, 2010; "Wind, Winter, Wendigo", *Unspeakable: A New Breed of Terror,* ed. Theresa Dillon, Blood Bound Books, 2010; "Transformations", *Don't Tread on Me: Tales of Revenge and Retribution*, ed. Gregory Miller, Static Movement, 2010; "Incident on Alkali Road" published with the title "Beneath Kent's Bed", *The Middle of Nowhere: Horror in Rural America,* Pill Hill Press, ed. Jessy Marie Roberts, 2009; "The Red Patch in the Snow", *Seasons in the Abyss,* ed. Jack Burton, Blood Bound Books, 2011; "The Restoration Room", *Gone With the Dirt: Undead Dixie,* ed. Jessy Marie Roberts, Pill Hill Press, 2010; "You Don't Know Jack", *Crossed Genres*, eds. Bart Leib and K.T. Holt, 2009; "The Artist and His Subject", *D.O.A.: Extreme Horror*, eds. David C. Hayes and Jack Burton, Blood Bound Books, 2011; "A Story About Monsters", "A Good Game", and "Solitary Man" published in issues 4, 9, and 15, respectively, *Morpheus Tales;* ed. Adam Bradley, 2010-11, "The Biggin Hill Duel" published in *Big Pulp: The Biggin Hill Duel*, ed. Bill Oyler, Spring 2012. Thanks to all these editors for selecting my work.

The stories included differ from the versions originally published. Edits, corrections and revisions have been made throughout.

ABOUT THE AUTHOR

ADRIAN LUDENS is a member of the Horror Writers Association. He lives and works in the Black Hills of South Dakota. Among his magazine appearances are *Alfred Hitchcock's Mystery Magazine* (two-time winner of their "Mysterious Photograph" story contest), a cover story for *Big Pulp* and three entries in *Morpheus Tales*. Recent anthology appearances include *Blood Rites* (Blood Bound Books), *Blood Lite III: Aftertaste* (Pocket Books), *Slices of Flesh* (Dark Moon Books), *Zombie Kong* (Books of the Dead Press) and *The Mothman Files* (Woodland Press). Adrian's author page on Amazon shows a number of other available titles.

Visit Adrian at:
*curiodities**adrianludens**.blogspot.com/*

Made in the USA
Charleston, SC
21 September 2012